Ghost Orchid

D.K. Christi

L & L Dreamspell
Spring, Texas

Cover and Interior Design by L & L Dreamspell

This is a work of fiction, and is produced from the author's imagination. People, places and things mentioned in this novel are
used in a fictional manner.

ISBN: 978-1-60318-136-5

Library of Congress Control Number: 2009933950

Visit us on the web at www.lldreamspell.com

Published by L & L Dreamspell
Printed in the United States of America

Acknowledgements

I must first thank the Audubon Corkscrew Swamp Sanctuary director and staff for the wonderful retreat where my soul is free to feel the beauty of nature and express itself through writing. Next, I want to thank my mother, Lueneda Johnson, for her patience with me when I bury myself in writing during her visits to Florida. Not only is she patient, but she is also my publicist, charming book store and festival patrons with her southern graciousness when I'm signing books and talking about my writing. From her, I inherited a romantic spirit that sees love all around. My friend Judy Schuitema continues to read and comment on my manuscripts for which I am grateful. I also want to thank the L & L Dreamspell editor, Cindy Davis, who knew just the right words to touch and improve my own voice. I have dedicated this book to my muse, who also reads every word and touches not only my manuscripts and makes them better, but also touches my heart.

Dedication

To my muse, the love of my life, keeper of
my heart, without whom no words would
be written, no stories would be told.

One
The Curve

The high-pitched, grating sound of twisting metal chased screaming birds into the sky. A sickening rumble erupted as the car dove into the earth, upside down, crushing the roof. The screeching tires etched black marks on the highway for several yards, carving trenches in the shoulder as the vehicles left the road. The bright, red sports car glanced off the white sedan, but slid safely along the edge of the blacktop and stopped just short of the ditch. A plume of smoke and dust almost concealed the careening vehicles.

The shocked dump truck driver, pulling a heavy load of gravel, lost control and the truck slammed into the ditch on the other side of the narrow two-lane highway, the impact jamming the doors shut. For a moment in time, a deafening silence filled the air as though the crash sucked the life out of the universe in exchange for the life of the driver who attempted the left turn from the sanctuary road. Her car was upside down across the ditch, her bleeding torso visible half out the window, suspended by the hanging seat belt and the deflating airbags.

The contents of the car—shoes, a jacket, a briefcase, a computer—flew with abandon across the field as the doors popped open on impact with the red car and the final slam into the earth. A silver disk hung precariously from the player slot, the music from his heart collected just for her now useless, empty. The cell phone that was in her hand at impact flew out the window and found its resting place in a clump of brush, well hidden from the carnage. In that split second, in a blink of the eye, a snap of the fingers, the time it takes for a sip of coffee, to change a computer disc, or to glance out the window; in that split second, she was gone. All that remained was a broken shell of the person who just moments ago validated life in her beloved sanctuary, the sanctuary where her heart resonated with nature, transforming all the doubts in her life into new hopes and longings just beyond her reach.

The dazed truck driver tumbled out, hitting the ground awkwardly as the door broke loose. Landing hard at first, he seemed unharmed. The driver of the red sports car ran toward the overturned sedan; but the truck driver, reaching for his fire extinguisher, dialing 911 on his cell phone at the same time, stopped him. He pointed to the raw fuel that poured down the side of the overturned car, filling the air with its ominous odor. Traffic stopped. A few people dashed from their vehicles in useless attempts to help, some to gawk. The site was terrifying: the tires still spinning in the air, the blood still oozing from the lifeless body, and the growing pool of potentially explosive fuel spreading ominously.

Everything that mattered before was no longer of any consequence: not the important papers that blew down the highway or the projects on the computer or the lists of things undone or the secrets that would never be revealed. Death was like that; or is it?

Two
Suspended in Time

At precisely 12:00 p.m., the middle aged woman in the third office pulled her chair back, logged off the computer, picked up her small purse with the long, thick strap and a bottle of water and left the room. She walked into the sunshine, away from the old and decaying building. The heat was shocking at first, even though she dressed casually in linen slacks and a white, cotton blouse. She hurried to the main office and signed the log, "Twelve fifteen, lunch."

She smiled at the office manager, "See you after my walk," she called over her shoulder, anxious to start the best part of her day.

The younger woman grumbled to herself, "She'll be late again," and followed with her eyes, thinking how old and tired the woman looked as she walked through the grass and dirt to her ancient automobile, coated in dust.

"I'll never look like that." She sighed, glancing at her own youthful vision in the mirror next to her desk.

The automobile engine's smooth hum was a welcome sound, and the steady flow of cool air chased the heat from the car as the hairline around her face released a few droplets of sweat. Backing out, she drove through the opening in the chain link fence past the tiny migrant housing shacks hidden from the highway by a picket fence, but visible from this access road. A ditch full of filthy water and flotsam followed the narrow road. Apparently, the cranes, ibis and egrets did not notice the filth, but rather appreciated the bits of food they found during the drought. They had wandered astray from the swamp. The family of alligators left in search of water also. She smiled at the memory of baby alligators riding on their mother's back. The graceful birds looked out of place here, just like her.

She turned right onto the two-lane highway, just like every other day at 12:20 p.m., and set the cruise control for 56 miles per hour, a necessity since the day the Sheriff's Deputy stopped her for driving twenty miles over the speed limit and gave her an official warning instead of a ticket. She always hurried to keep her lunch within one hour; but now she still completed her walks, late returning or not. She had driven much too fast for the dangerous, two-lane highway, but now used caution, since the near ticket. A ticket was such a waste of hard earned money.

Another right turn led her into the swamp, just as it had for several years, where she still looked for the parking spot under the tree at the far end of the lot with a bit of shade, knowing that by the time her walk ended, the sun would be beating on her car, searching for things to melt. She parked in the end spot with sprigs of shade, right next to the staff parking sign. She tucked her long hair, streaked with gray, inside a wide-brimmed cap, catching a glimpse of herself in the rear view mirror as she adjusted her one splurge, the stylish sunglasses. She smiled. They hid the deepening crinkles around her eyes and the furrow between her brows. Otherwise, she was lucky that her complexion remained smooth with a youthful glow.

Whooping crane feet and bear paws were stamped into the cement walk to the main building for the little ones to follow toward their adventure. She followed the bear paws, still smiling at the kid in her that enjoyed the imagined tracking. A blast of cool air greeted her as she entered through the double doors of the main building. To the right was a small café, to the left, a gift shop. She already passed the metal sculpture with wood storks feeding and the giant map of the bird sanctuary trails sanctioned by the Audubon Society.

"Well, hello." The elderly guard with the very southern accent, standing at the centrally located reception desk, greeted her with a smile. He wore crisp khakis; his white hair was trimmed neatly, and a tidy white mustache finished off the combination that possibly made him appear older than his age. She'd passed through his gate for many years. His wife started a new diet. He recently recovered from surgery. He liked his job. He might take a class at her school sometime. This day, he was engrossed in a book to which he returned before she could respond to his perfunctory greeting. They had a relationship, she and the elderly guard. They said "hello" nearly five days a week. When he was not there, and a stranger occupied his place, the day felt a bit off. She wondered if he noticed when she did not pass by the desk. She had an annual membership. She really did not need to stop.

Her face softened and filled with a glowing smile as she walked through the cool building into the hot day and the beginning of her official walk. Some days she and the guide had long conversations. He read her published stories and had plenty to say about the morals portrayed in some of them. It was a good thing she wrote fiction. He might not let her in the park. Each day when he read a new story, he quizzed her about the decisions made by the heroine, asking, "What's next?" Of course, she did not tell him. His smile was particularly charming then, attempting to coax an answer from her.

Today was hot. It was so hot it took her breath away. Likely the temperature was ninety-eight degrees or so; but the humidity was equally high, weighing heavily on her chest as she started her brisk walk. She breathed deep and slow, making certain she did not panic. She believed she had beaten the life-threatening asthma that reached into her lungs and robbed her of many enjoyable activities recently, a time when she felt like she was drowning and life might be slipping away. The diagnosis, "occupational asthma," was caused by the ancient and unkempt building where bats made their home in the roof, asbestos was a primary building material and mold and mildew lurked beneath new paint. The fate of its occupants was of little concern to their supervision.

The building was "condemned" and received little attention and certainly no expensive repairs or maintenance. After all, she should be able to find a job elsewhere if it was that bad. When she felt the heaviness grow in her chest and the labored breathing began, she started counting, "One, two, three, four," telling her mind to relax the muscles so the lungs could function more efficiently. It seemed to work. Like the building, she was also condemned.

The bulletin board had only a few cards marked. Earlier visitors posted little cards that displayed the plants and animals they identified on their visit. She scanned the board to see if anyone saw a bear or a deer. The swamp was hot and dry; many of the animals moved elsewhere in search of water. Yet, the miracle of life continued to spring forth with new surprises; some of the smaller animals stayed here like the locals who enjoyed the hot summers, the easy pace and the lack of traffic. Perhaps, like her, they had nowhere else to go.

Ahead, a little squirrel ran along the railing at the edge of the boardwalk, looking back to see if she was chasing along behind. For a few minutes, she felt like she had a companion.

"Don't run away," she said to the squirrel. "I am harmless." She laughed as the animal leaped from the rail to a tree, just barely catching the limb. It looked back at her and chattered as if to tell her that she had interfered with plans. Laughter was the balm of the soul.

"Oh my!" escaped from her lips with an audible sigh. "God must have spilled a bucket of whitewash to cover the entire marsh with white cymbidium, floating on slender stems in the weak breeze." She stood in wonder, gazing across the marsh, the cypress swamp bidding her to hurry onward. She fantasized leaving the fenced boardwalk to dance through the flowers, but continued toward the cypress instead.

Little red cardinals darted among the newly budding cypress leaves, their feathers even brighter with so few other blooming plants with which to compete. Only the white cymbidium found enough moisture to thrive. The redheaded woodpeckers were having a convention; two and three hammered on the same spreading trees. She heard an alligator with its deep-throated, grumbling sound in the distance, keeping time with the gruff bullfrogs. A little further down the path she slowed her pace, in awe of the barrel owl just overhead.

"If I had been walking a little faster, I would have missed you entirely!"

These were her friends, her companions during her afternoon walks. She spoke with them as though they would respond to her inquiries.

She stopped and the two of them stared at each other. She began her journey again, strolling down the path. Glancing back, she saw the owl following her with its head moving around on its perfectly still body, the eyes glued on her, piercing and watchful.

After she passed, she heard another owl calling "Whooooooo?" from deep in the swamp; and she recognized her owl answering. She smiled and commented to the quiet vastness of the swamp,

"Ah hah, so you have a mate."

The little anoles were every color on this day, black and brown and green. One day she saw one changing color, mesmerized by the miracle. Another squirrel decided to join her. They were the least timid, apparently enjoying the company of those who walked along the boardwalk. A solitary, bright red swamp hibiscus, surrounded by gigantic ferns and alligator flags; its five large red petals on a tall, too-thin stem, bobbing a little in the swamp breeze seemed to say, "See, I am still here."

Paper white cymbidiums and a white swamp lily or two were also dressed in their finest. The more she looked, the more flowers she saw. The purple morning glories were still partially open. Tall ferns, reminiscent of the age of dinosaurs, rose from the dry swamp floor, surrounded by other broad leaf, alligator plants, trying to catch a little dew and a wisp of sunshine. The mysteries of the swamp were like a well in a story she loved, beautiful because they were initially hidden, just waiting for the right conditions for their dramatic entrance. Some pine tree seeds only opened after a fire cleared the way, dormant for years. Thus, the Everglades were always beautiful for two reasons, what was seen and what was left to the imagination, waiting to burst forth in the future.

The swamp was the coolest place she knew this time of year. Even on the hottest and most humid day, a little swamp breeze wafted through the trees, rustled the dry leaves and cooled the sweat on her face and arms. Her hat acted like a sweatband, stopping the salty, pooling drops from slipping down her forehead and into her eyes. She loved the winding boardwalk where she threw her shoulders back, looked up into the green canopy overhead that provided some shade and did not miss a step on her brisk walk. She breathed in the oxygen, knowing her lungs were saying thank you with every step.

One thing she knew about walking in the swamp: she did not cry. An overwhelming sense of peace filled her heart to overflowing with joy from the first step into its wonders until the last step out. Tears were for lonely automobiles, the back of the church, the empty rooms. Her Creator who made this swamp such a beautiful and serene place where nature lived in harmony according to its predestined imprint had done no less for her. In the swamp, she felt her God filling the void in her soul; and she was at peace. This walk was the highlight of her day, a raison d'être for the long drive to a job that lost its spark with an accumulation of career disappointments. The swamp never disappointed.

Thunder began as a rumble in the distance but rolled forward with loud crashes. Lightning soon followed across the sky, long, jagged lines of white light connecting the growing cumulus clouds with the earth. These bolts of lightning were frightening this time of year. They started the unmanageable fires in the swamplands that filled the air with acrid smoke and threatened the homes of those who ventured too far into the wilderness. The heavy wind howled through the cypress; and heavy rains broke through the canopy, dancing on the wide alligator fronds and turning the moss covered walk to "swamp ice." The initial raindrops glanced off her hat brim as she quickened her step. She enjoyed the warm, summer rain. The air was alive with the crackling lightning, and she counted in her mind's eye how far it was to the next protected area to possibly wait it out. Wet, her blouse clung revealingly to her skin, the cool dampness uncomfortable.

Just as quickly as the storm arrived, it passed away. The sun returned in all its hot glory; diamonds glistened on the broad, deep green fronds and cool drops still fell from the canopy overhead. She was cool and wet, but she would dry by the time the walk ended so she could return to work with no one knowing she came through a storm. Her recent hairstyle was straight with short bangs cut across her forehead. She wore little makeup to wash away in the rain. The main disaster was the shoes. The damp leather soles sloshed through the rain, traversing the slick pine needles; they might even separate from the straps. This happened before. The swamp was the dividing line between before and after.

Before, she talked for the entire walk with the man who resided in her heart. She shared the serenity, the pure joy of this special place that meant so much to her. In spite of the "no cell phone" rule, she was eager for his calls that he actually timed for her walks in the swamp. Perhaps for him it meant she had private time to chat, away from the office, just the two of them. She found a bench off the beaten path to be away from the occasional patrons who might give her the evil eye for whispering into a cell phone.

A radiant smile filled her face the whole time, heart racing, heat rising. He had that power over her. He was "the one," the soul mate for whom nothing was sacrosanct, except for her painful secret, buried too deep to reveal. They were of one mind and heart, and her very essence with all its greatness and its flaws was safe with him. He would do her no more harm. As soon as their conversations ended, she thought about all the things she should have said or chided herself for talking too much, being too eager to share every thought with him to make up for all the years of separation.

Maybe I should have held back a few more secrets, she thought in the painful time that came after.

The walks were still the same. She passed the bench where they chatted, and for a fleeting moment her mind turned to him. She would not let it linger there. She was not a glutton for punishment. She understood at last that she was what she held in her thoughts. If she thought about the loss, then she felt the pain. She had experienced enough pain in her life; this was a time to reserve space for joy whenever possible. Wasting thoughts on a love gone sour took good space and turned it sour as well. She could not help but have a moment's passing thought, however, always a risk for tears.

Every ecstasy carries the risk of agony; at least I have known both. He meant so very much to me; surely loving him was not a mistake. She looked out across the swamp, watching the mist rise from the wet leaves, carried through the ferns and alligator flags on the gentle breeze. Life was as unpredictable as the storms and as mysterious as her little anole. She waited in anticipation; perhaps her beloved swamp would provide her the answers with which she could live.

Three
Neev

"Where is that man?" Neev half shouted and half exclaimed to no one in particular, standing in the heat and humidity watching for Roger. Their flight was quite uneventful; but his normally pleasant disposition was missing as they disembarked. This second flight was one flight too many. Neev barely spoke to him for the entire transatlantic flight and the short hop from New York. Perhaps more planning should have gone into this trip instead of the instant departure from Rome.

"There you are! I thought maybe this little airport had you fooled and you couldn't find me." Neev's impatience was well known among her friends. She was much too busy living to wait unnecessarily for anything from dinner reservations to boarding a plane or catching a taxi. She went to great lengths to avoid waiting at most any cost.

Her presence commanded attention that often made waiting moot anyway. People rushed to assist her. She was striking wherever she went. Her tall, lean body reached above six feet with a shock of bright red hair touching her shoulders, almost wild as it tried to escape from a black leather cap making an attempt to hold the hair in one place. Alabaster skin, penetrating hazel eyes that looked through long lashes, and a rash of freckles across her nose and cheeks from the unavoidable sun were just a few of her attributes. Her full mouth, with a careless blush of lipstick, was shaped in a pout and matched the frown between curving brows.

She paced back and forth on the serviceable pumps that gave her unneeded, additional height. A tight piece of leather skirt was wrapped around her slender hips; a white blouse, open in a deep "V" and tied just above her belly button, decorated with body jewelry, revealed surprisingly round breasts for her slender frame. A satin camisole fit loosely across her braless bosom, visible in the V of her blouse. Long, golden hoops hung in threes from her small ears, tucked close to her head. The hoops dangled as Neev walked, peeking from under the swinging red hair.

Long, slender arms were draped with a thin scarf that matched the camisole, a mannish watch graced her left wrist; no other jewelry adorned her frame. Neev had no time for jewelry that required changing or make-up either. Her youthful glow required nothing more than a little sun protection. Neev was a natural beauty, unaware of her attributes and the stares that followed her everywhere. She had more important things to accomplish in life than the few years she spent as a mannequin, gracing some of the best fashion openings in major shows across Europe. Now, long past her teens, she was too old anyway. She was grateful for the education at Oxford and the years traveling with National Geographic that gave her an appreciation for nature and the wonders revealed to her on every shoot.

Roger opened the door to the Kia Sportage, a fun rental car for their unexpected Florida adventure. He was uncharacteristically secretive about everything. Even though she traveled with a fashion shoot to New York and Los Angeles years ago, she acquired no great love for the United States, unlike many of her contemporaries. She preferred the anonymity of the Outback of Australia, the jungles of South America and the Veldts of South Africa. New York City was at least preferable to Los Angeles, that sprawling never-never land with no real city, only infinite freeways, the only routes to anywhere. Florida was never an option. Only Roger's insistence brought her to this harbinger of pain.

"Okay, Roger, it's time to tell me about the big secret that kept you so irritable for this whole trip. Since you received the ghost orchid picture for the Coffee Table book, you have been unbearable. It is beyond me how one picture could be so upsetting to you and drive you to kidnap me and bring me here to this humid and miserable place. We are missing a European autumn in exchange for these ugly palm trees and acres of cement and shrubs as far as I can see."

"Give us a chance, Neev. I promise you an experience you will not forget. Remember all the blooms that filled our cameras in the jungles of South Africa and Venezuela? Remember how you were swept away with their beauty? We have the opportunity to pursue our own quest. This may be the culmination of our years working together. It may be life changing. Trust me, please. Trust me once again."

Four
The Game

Roger and Neev settled into the Sportage and drove out of the airport toward the hotel. The Palmetto was everything Roger described and more. The turn from the highway led to a narrow, winding road to the hotel. A tower loomed at the end, reaching high into the blue sky, puffs of cloud wrapping around the turrets. Royal palms lined the sides of the road, like cement sentinels. They drove under the awning where formal attired valets whisked their luggage onto the cart for the equally formal bellmen.

The marble entry passed through enormous, carved, mahogany doors to the interior that mixed mahogany and rich, sparkling, gold-veined marble. Oversized vases, full of cut tropical blooms and foliage, deep reds, rich golds, burnt oranges and deep greens, sat as centerpieces on large, round tables, inlaid with crushed shells beneath smoked glass. Birds of paradise and bold, red-hot pokers took Neev back to the jungles, alive with vibrancy and color.

Living orchid plants decorated little tables in intimate seating areas around the edge of the lobby, separated with columns. The ceiling itself revealed deeply carved mahogany, the ever-present Bahamas fans whirling in synchronization. The ornate lobby reminded Neev of elegant ships that carried the wealthy across the Atlantic long before flight became pedestrian. The orchids were not nearly as haunting as the ghost orchid on the Coffee Table book, Roger's current obsession; yet, their delicate beauty called to her. She turned away as Roger approached registration.

"I have reservations for two rooms, Roger Andrew, on the concierge floor." The clerk behind the high, mahogany desk wasted no time with the folders, asking if they wanted to know anything in particular about the hotel.

"The ferry to the island leaves one more time today, just before sunset. The bus to the resort pools and amenities leaves every hour. A duo is playing in the lobby tonight, and I would be happy to make reservations for dinner. If there are any tours or places of interest you wish to explore, the Concierge can be very helpful."

The clerk continued with his litany of interesting points about the hotel. "A full spa is available; here is the list of services. One of our spa features is the mineral bath, warm minerals to heal the body while classical music plays beneath the surface. It is one of the spa favorites."

Neev could not hold back the mischievous smile that escaped her lips. She imagined the two of them floating in a mineral bath with Brahms playing. Perhaps a sunset cruise or a fine meal was possible; the spa was not.

"Thanks. For now, we'll just check out the rooms." Roger handed Neev her room key with a wry smile, took her elbow and guided her to the elevator.

The bellman already took the luggage, so it was waiting at their rooms. Neev wondered with some amusement which room had the luggage. This was how they traveled since first they met. They always had two rooms. The age difference between them often troubled Roger. He believed someday the miracle that brought them together would crash, and she would realize he was not a famous photographer but just an old man. The time was here.

He enjoyed his good fortune while he could. She was like the fountain of youth for him. He knew every curve of her body, every freckle, even those misplaced. When she touched him, the thrill was the only time that even perfection of light and subject took second place. She filled his mind and his heart so completely that sometimes he feared losing his passion for the wild, natural world in exchange for the passion he held for Neev. Now, those passionate days were drawing to a close.

Neev had never known anyone like Roger. Her few experiences with men over the years were quite disappointing. They generally were so mesmerized by her striking features that they never bothered to find out who she was, to discover the lonely young woman with a gaping hole in her heart, the girl whose mother gave her away to the loving care of friends in Germany and left her to rot in boarding schools in Europe. She overcame her abandonment with a fierce individualism that gave her an aura of self-confidence that was only pierced by the men who craved her beauty and sexuality but not her heart.

How could a mother leave her child thousands of miles away and see her once or twice a year? When Neev was old enough to realize that Truse and Rolf were not her parents but rather dear friends of her mother's, she was old enough to begin hating her mother. One day her mother sent her the gift: a camera. Her mother thought the camera might encourage Neev to send pictures, a glimpse of the little girl's childhood that she denied herself. She waited in vain; there were no pictures sent to the mother.

The camera became Neev's constant companion, her mother-substitute, her friend. She took pictures of the world around her, but not to send her mother in the States. She developed her own black and white photographs that her wonderful German family framed and hung throughout their home, changing them through the years as Neev received her education at the best boarding schools until she was "discovered" while drinking tea at an outdoor table in Paris with classmates. She was 14 years young, on holiday with her friends and their tutor. The girls wore matching, checkered school uniforms; but anyone could see Neev as the natural beauty among them. Nothing could disguise the unruly hair and biting hazel eyes that pierced into the psyche and stole hearts.

She called her mother in America to tell her about the chance to model, to invite her to meet the agency owner. Instead, her mother hired an attorney to write the power of attorney for Truse and Rolf to be certain that Neev was not exploited. Neev studied and modeled in one continuous whirlwind around the globe for the next four years. Unlike the other models, she preferred looking through the camera, not into it. She took no joy in the wealth and excitement, the lives of the rich and famous. The raw, sexual aura that reached out from the fashion shows and the photographs was pure acting for Neev, her emotions uninvolved.

This was just another game for her, a time-consuming game until her real life could begin. One day on a London shoot, she found a solicitor who worked out a release from her contract; and she studied at Oxford instead, majoring in philosophy. She liked the intellectual challenge. She did not need her mother's money any more; she saved from her modeling years and invested well. She spent semester breaks with friends, traveling wherever the spirit took them, always taking pictures. Her dissertation connected philosophy and art, specifically the art of capturing that special moment in the natural world when light and subject were perfect.

Her own perfect day came when National Geographic hired her to accompany a famous Florida photographer on a shoot deep into the jungles of South America to capture flowers that grew nowhere else in the world, some nearing extinction. She recognized his name, Roger Andrew. She had admired his work for years. He was best known for his Florida Everglades photography, one of the few places she had never visited. Her estrangement from her mother kept her from wanting to visit the United States. Her mother came to see her in New York and Los Angeles when she was modeling, but their time together was strained and ended with harsh words.

"If you can't love me, then, tell me about my father's family. Surely they aren't all dead as well? I want to know about the parts of me that are nothing like you, most of me I believe. I do not look like you at all except for the shape of my eyes and my long, skinny arms. Who do I look like? Do I look like my father? Why are he and his family such a dark secret? I have a right to know my roots. Why do you deny them to me?" Neev always pulled the "father card" to be sure any time spent with her mother ended in anger. It made the parting easier to tolerate.

That was the last time she saw her mother. Now, she was truly an orphan, an adult orphan whose German family was now all she had in the world; and they were so good to her that she abandoned the one unsuccessful attempt to get information from them. Their love, however, was not sufficient to quell the unanswered questions, the mystery of her parentage. Now, the answers were as lost to her as the reconciliation with her mother.

Five
The Swamp's Promise

The one reward from the long drive to and from the office was the daily walk in the swamp. She tried to be philosophical about the change in her life, the emptiness it brought that even the swamp could not dispel. She still rode her bike to church every Sunday. Repeated patterns helped her stay focused. Every day she drove the dangerous two-lane road to her work site and put in a reasonable day's activities. She knew her responsibilities so well that little effort was required. The afternoon at the office was bearable after the walk in the Everglades.

Some days, she drove home in the evening on the winding road through the Everglades. Those days, she slipped into her swimsuit and a little cover-up and rode her bike to the nearby pool for her excuse for laps. She also enjoyed the beach, especially when the tide was out. The hot Gulf waters were not as refreshing as the pool. She floated in the ninety degree sea, almost like floating in air with water and air the same temperature as the body; she emptied her mind except for the changing shapes in the clouds. She floated there until awakened to the fear of sunburn or a fish nibbled on her heel or a breeze stirred up a ruffle on the water. *Maybe death is like this, the absence of body or thought, just floating in warmth and simplicity, back to the womb from which we originated.* Floating in the hot sea felt magical as she watched gulls fly across the sun.

On the days she drove home in the other direction, on the newly widened road past gated communities and expanding townhouse and condo developments that filled the former gravel pits, she stopped at a few stores for groceries or even a bookstore to see how her stories were selling or to set up another event.

At first, she was just grateful to see her published stories in bookstores. She felt compelled to finish her novel in fear that a hurricane would carry away all the research she had completed, especially during one bad year with several dangerous storms. Once she was under contract with a publisher, it was mandatory to finish based on their inflexible timelines. She had to finish in a matter of months the work of her lifetime, the stories of herself, camouflaged in fiction. When the stories were truly in print, she was terrified at the revelations in the writing. Yet, she was obsessed with finishing. She was driven. The purpose was in finishing; there was no other design. Between the covers were all the bits of paper, hopes and dreams dashed, vignettes of joy, mementos and memories that spread through her house and her life like insidious little monsters sapping her strength as she gathered them up, preserved them and moved them to the next chapter in her own life. She kept one secret to herself; it would not be revealed in fiction. The life's journey was complete with that exception.

Always respecting symbolism, she had an eerie sensation that finishing the stories would close her life, and death would be eminent. She accepted this inevitability with amazing calm. At least no one would face the daunting task of sorting through her boxes of memories; or worse, simply dumping them all unceremoniously into the trash bin. No one would find the hidden secrets that didn't make the pages of her books and stories, the ones that would never see the light of day. With the stories written, she could throw the telltale papers away, all but a few treasured mementos and one letter carefully put away in a small box, the only evidence of that hidden part of her soul that cried to be heard.

Six
Time

Neev learned of her mother's death too late. Time for travel to the United States for proper grieving was gone. She did grieve. At one moment she was an eighteen year old girl walking down a Los Angeles fashion ramp with a beaming mother in the audience; at another, they were in their locked anger; at another, a deep emptiness swallowed her in depression, missing the years that should have been spent with her mother, hating herself for staying angry, ripping up her mother's letters, changing her cell phone numbers, changing addresses.

In her grief, Neev considered for the first time that her mother must have lived a strange and lonely life. Neev did not understand why. Her mother was almost a recluse from the best Neev could tell, working at a nondescript job, writing short stories that Neev discovered every now and then on the Internet. Sometimes, Neev was poised at the computer, ready to send off an email to her mother, to tell her how a story had touched her heart; but her anger would stop her. Truse and Rolf in Germany were her mother and father. They were aging; she had to be there for them when she could.

During those times when her anger was at its peak, she hungered to find her father's family. She held a fantasy that he might still be alive, that his death was a fabrication. Sometimes, on a photo shoot in some exotic, global location, she would see a man who looked like she imagined her father. Once, in France, she saw a man in a U.S. military uniform that was almost like seeing an older version of her in a mirror. Neev wanted to run up to him and ask his name and where he was from. She knew it was foolish. She smiled in the camera, watching him from the corner of her eye. She thought for a moment that he was moving in her direction, but he turned and walked away. She still had one of those pictures as a reminder of the day she thought she saw her father.

Another time in Los Angeles, Neev was shopping in Nordstrom's after a particularly difficult quarrel with her mother who had come to watch her fashion shoot. An older man with tipped cap, much like those she favored, was shopping for gloves. His blue eyes caught hers for just a moment, almost quizzical, almost a sign of recognition. The moment passed.

What if that was my father? She mused in her youthful fantasy. Over the years, she picked out men in the distance and imagined a story around them, a story of how they left her and her mother and would be returning to claim her. Of course, it was only a game. Her father was dead; her mother would never reveal anything about him. It was a wasted game.

Okay, Neev, step out of your daydream and pick your room. This was another game she and Roger played, the two-room game. Well, Roger insisted, and Neev acquiesced. She once loved their nights together, always a choice, not an expectation. Roger was a thoughtful and gentle lover, not like the selfish men she had known on her few adventures with romance. She always felt superior in some way to the men her age with their high impressions of their own prowess as lovers. She watched too many courting animals in the jungle to believe "that's all there is" to the bedroom antics of her ill-fated romances.

Neev poured her passions into her photographs. Her meeting with Roger, though, was a high point in her young life. Sometimes, when she relived the wild days in Africa not too long ago, she had guilt pangs about the ill-fated affair with Gunhart, the German guide who wrapped her in his own excitement with the hunt, the raw animal passion of Africa. She never loved Gunhart any more than he loved her. They were like the very animals they followed, raw instinct without connection, brave and daring. In some dark way, Neev suspected that Africa was a purposeful attempt to hurt Roger, to punish him for loving her unconditionally. She had to hurt those she loved to make up for those who were supposed to love her and caused pain instead. It didn't make any sense. Gunhart was a passing fling, an experiment that failed.

Seven
Dust to Dust

The walk in the Everglades slipped into that dangerous zone of reverie. Her system for surviving disappointments forced her to live in the moment. This philosophy of the moment caused a bit of conflict recently. He was a planner. Of course, she was once a captive of planning also. Her entire life was planned out as a young woman, and she believed she took the right steps to get there. The future held nothing but promise in her youth.

Plans fell flat, dreams dissipating into thin air. All the planning for future goals gave her nothing better than what she fell into with no effort. The difference? Living in the moment allowed for few expectations and prevented disappointments when they did not materialize. Her life was no longer an emotional roller coaster. She did cry for about a week when this single slip into expectation once again bit her. She wrote him twenty-six unsent emails full of anger and pain, and then she stopped. One week of mourning was sufficient.

"Whew! These pine needles are really slippery!" she exclaimed as she caught herself before a free-fall on the boardwalk. It reminded her of the fact that love itself was a slippery slope. Once the sliding began, stopping was difficult until slammed into a wall. The agony often felt unbearable. All the little things that meant so much became meaningless. Unless the thoughts were shared, little secrets that once led to secretive smiles fell flat. The mementos no longer represented the person in the present that claimed his undying love and forever caring in the past. The poetry from a previously loving heart no longer rhymed. The seashells collected for their perfection, representing their love, were just empty remnants of their former inhabitants.

It was like walking through a door that slammed shut, forever. Whatever lay on the other side was gone! The sound of the slamming door cut like a knife through the heart, carving out all that was previously dear and intimate, leaving a sordid mess of jumbled feelings with no place to escape, left to fester and rot. It seemed amazing that life continued. The shared world came to an end, and life was suddenly thrust back into the same patterns she followed most days; yet, nothing was the same. That's how it was all those painful years ago when her youth became bitter and angry; that's how it was today though she learned to be more accepting, to release the anger, not to harbor bitterness. She accepted reality these days. She reached for serenity. She found her vignettes of joy in the moment.

She chose a different return path with more shade and passed the same guide she saw on this path most days. His sun hat was jauntily perched on his head; the strings dangled on either side. He was quite tall with a clean-shaven face and wearing tidy khakis. He smiled the same as always and tipped his hat in recognition. The true fanatics didn't talk in the swamp; they did not want to disturb the wildlife. The swamp guides were volunteers, mostly older, retired or independently wealthy people. They participated in bird watches and set up cameras for the novices to see the owl perched high above or the woodpecker or the baby eaglets in their nest. She considered volunteering some day when she had time. If she forgot to remove her work identification tag, visitors often asked questions as though she was a guide already. Sometimes, she had answers for the curious.

Will they see an alligator?

"In the winter, the Audubon Society pays one old ten-foot alligator to pose on that log over there so you can take his picture. He has summers off, however."

That was always good for a laugh. If they were English or

Canadian, their laughter sometimes came slower as they pondered the reasonableness of what she told them. Or they might say, "I saw nothing in the swamp. When will I see something?"

She wanted to tell them to open their eyes and they would see everything. But she just smiled and suggested they listen for the sounds instead of worrying about what they saw. Once they started listening, they often began to see.

That's when it hit her, when she started to listen. It happened so very quickly, it snuck up on her; she was only slightly aware that it was beginning. The glow she had been wearing started to dim. The sparkle in her eyes started to disappear. The sway in her hips, the chin tilted up, the shoulders thrown back all slipped a little. The excitement that exuded from every pore in her body dissipated, evidenced by the less flirtatious smiles around her and her own lack of interest in theirs. Oh, everything was okay, just like before. She woke, she dressed, she drove to work, she walked in the swamp, she talked with her friends, she planned her vacation, she took on a new work project, she cried to the oldies but goodies, and she watched for his blip, held her cell phone to her heart to force its ring. It rang: Marie, her dentist that she had been ignoring.

Nearing the end of the walk and leaving the serenity of the swamp, she looked at the controlled burn area; the charred remains of trees and shrubs were now overgrown with spreading, purple morning glories. This was where she wanted her ashes scattered so her spirit could mix with the earth and blend her life force with the cycle of life that existed in this marvelous place for over 600 years. Six hundred years was long enough. That was the age of the oldest cypress there. Her ashes in this place would be protected as they worked their way through the cycle of living flora and fauna. No houses or streets would ever take this land from the Audubon Society. Too many endangered species found their home in this swamp in one season or another. Here, her spirit would be free.

She fit well, as unique as her surroundings. "Please let me

love someone else," she prayed to the earth goddess.

She used to pray, "Let me be in his arms just once more before I die," until they recently found each other, and he left her again.

"Let me love someone else, please," became her new prayer. "Let me want to be touched by someone else. Remove the curse that ties me to this man alone. Drop into my life someone who needs me, whose life is complete but whose heart aches for a mate and finds mine compatible. Give me someone whose touch excites instead of repulses; someone whose smile lights my soul and puts life in my steps and songs in my voice; someone for whom loving me is the priority over all life's gifts as I return the same; someone who will walk into eternity by my side in spirit and wonder, hand in mine, loving all the way; someone to share my tears and laughter, my fun and frolic, my losses and sorrows, my ecstasies and agonies."

She knew, however, that she made her deal with the devil many years ago. She loved this man with the essence of her being, leaving her an empty shell when he left her, forever hungering for his return to fill her again, to claim his gift. Did he actually return? Or was it just one more fantasy in her life of imagination? Was it just a story she wrote to reflect the longing in her soul? There was no other mate for her. She was not unique in this way. Other species mate for life. They are her kin. In spite of the swamp's power, one last tear gathered in the corner of her eye as the owl called, "Whoooo?" There had always been only one answer for her.

"Come again," the kindly guard called after her as she left through the building for the parking lot, smiling once again at the prints from the whooping crane and the bear. The car baked in the sun, over a hundred degrees inside. She removed her hat; her long, brunette hair with a touch of red highlights fell to her shoulders, damp from the sweat. She was grateful for the weight loss and exercise that was evident in the fit of her clothes and her quick movements. She took a couple drinks from her water bottle as she waited for the car to cool a little. The oldies but goodies played on 106.3.

"Until the twelfth of never..." She slipped into the seat and moved the channel selection to National Public Radio for a good dose of classical music. She would not cry in her car today! The burst of cool air, finally, was welcome as she drove from the sanctuary parking lot and stopped at the highway for her left turn. She was running late as usual. She looked to the left and to the right, waiting for the traffic to clear.

Eight
In The Beginning

"So, you are my other half for this journey! You look a little frail to me. Are you accustomed to the hardships we will endure? We will leave the comforts of home far behind. Aren't you a little afraid to start off on this adventure with a lecherous old man like me?"

That was how Roger greeted Neev at the airport after she disembarked in Caracas. The deep jungle, another airplane ride and a hike with bearers, was yet ahead of them. Neev had garnered this great assignment with National Geographic, a rare opportunity for a neophyte photographer. She was accompanying the famous Roger Andrew on a shoot to capture rare and endangered flowers in the jungles of Venezuela before they became extinct. This was the break she had been working toward since leaving Oxford and striking out as a freelance photographer.

"Only you know whether you're a risk, but there's a lot of karate in this frail body of mine; and in my more frivolous youth, I backpacked through Asia where white girls, especially one with red hair and six feet tall, were a shocking novelty. Locals left their earthen homes to stare and giggle and share their meager suppers with us. We slept in rice patties and mountain caves. Sometimes the missionaries took pity, and we had a good shower and a real meal. I think I can manage the deprivations associated with a National Geographic shoot. What do you think?" And she smiled at him with those eyes that read his heart and saw only kindness there, none of the threats he promised.

"Well, let's get going then. We will have our last comfortable night in a lodge at the edge of the jungle; then we will board a riverboat. After that, we will use blowup kayaks, but we will have bearers to help us until we reach the river. Any questions?"

He looked as though he genuinely expected her to ask something. She had questions, all right, but they were questions about him. She knew he was in his sixties; yet, he appeared years younger. He had the physique of a younger man, dressed in blue jeans and a white T-shirt that revealed muscular arms with a deep tan. He might be described as slender himself, almost too thin. His deeply tanned face hid the furrows and lines from a life in the elements. He had a full head of dark, wavy hair, just a touch too long, and a neatly trimmed beard with touches of gray mixed in at his temples, a hint of his real age. He had a commanding way about him that she liked. Without question, he was in charge of this expedition, and she had better settle into that understanding and quickly.

"So," he talked as they hurried to their next plane, "what family are you leaving behind for this great adventure for National Geographic?"

"Absolutely none. My foster family is in Germany, but they suffered my youth and learned not to worry. I have few other relatives, and my friends are faithful enough to follow me by email and forgive me my long absences. I do worry a little about Truse and Rolf sometimes; but other than that, what you see is what I have." Neev gave her family history with humor, but the pain of the few relatives in her life ran deep. "You know my story; what's yours?"

"My wife left me years ago...with good reason. I was gone more than home, finding my passion in my work, not in my family. I have a son and a daughter who hold me in the same poor regard as their mother. We get together now and then, but I'm always happy to run away to jungles, deserts and swamps, to the forgiving regeneration of nature. There, I understand the rules. They fit with my nature. I guess we will make a cheery pair!" He laughed, putting an end to the disintegrating conversation.

They boarded their plane, an older Boeing 707, releasing their backpacks to the baggage personnel. Tired, they both fell sound asleep. Her red head rested on his shoulder, comfortable, safe. She looked pale next to his weathered face as she slept peacefully, barely disturbed as the plane bounced across the poorly maintained runway as it landed.

"Wake up sleepyhead," Roger moved the hair from across her face that had drifted there during their flight. "You are lucky you missed the landing. I thought we were going off the edge of the plateau. Take a look out the window. It appears as though we have taxied to the end of the world."

Neev looked. He was right. She looked beyond the edge, the jungle spreading out in the distance, bathed in the twilight of the setting sun. She shuddered a little. This might be more adventure than she planned.

"Okay, let's go see what we have for accommodations." She followed Roger off the plane, already dependent on his leadership after knowing him for less than twenty-four hours. She felt protected.

The lodge was located at the edge of the jungle all right. Much too open for her taste: no locks on the doors, no air conditioning, just lots of screened openings with whirling Bahamas fans overhead. Adjoining rooms gave Neev some comfort, but anxiety built in the pit of her stomach. Once they settled into their rooms, the world around them turned pitch black. The only lights were the hurricane lamps for this electric-free dwelling. Instead of a romantic glow, the lights flickered and cast sinister shadows across the walls and ceiling.

Cheerful adventurers filled the dining hall, many from down under, thick with Australian accents. *It must be a tour group*, thought Neev. Her prep school education gave her perfect diction and a mastery of linguistics that guaranteed her speech fell somewhere between British and American with no particular accent noticeable. She was fluent in Italian, French, several German dialects, and enough Spanish to be dangerous. Roger counted on her Spanish to help with this trip. He admitted he spoke only a little himself, picked up among the migrant workers in Florida. It was Mexican Spanish, another language compared to the Spanish spoken in Venezuela.

Screams pierced the night. Neev sat in the middle of her bed, bathed in a little light from the dying kerosene lamp, dressed in a sheer, white sleeping gown, her slender body showing through, her breasts high and heaving as she continued the non-stop screaming. Finally, she saw Roger flying through the doorway. The source of her terror, twelve inches from her hunched up body: a small python, coiled and looking at her. They seemed to be in a stare-off. Before Roger could act, a security guard burst into the room, gun and net in hand. In one swift motion, he threw the net over the snake, and the apparition in the center of the bed flew across the room, huddling on the floor in the corner, sobbing. Roger rushed to her, wrapped her in a bear hug and held her until her sobs subsided and her trembling body's shaking stopped. Where the snake and its captor disappeared, remained unknown.

"Hey now, Neev, let's calm down and think about this situation. The floor is likely the worst place for us under these circumstances. How about you coming with me to my room? We'll light up another lamp, sit on my settee, and have a good stiff drink while you tell me where you got the name Neev, a name I have never heard before. What do you think of that idea?"

Neev stopped shaking, but still could not answer. She reveled in the safety of Roger's strong arms in this moment of fear. She wanted the safety of those arms to continue. She glanced across the room at the bed. "No, I don't want to sit on any settee and think about that creature all night. I want you to take me into your bed and hold me tight; protect me from any more terrors in the night."

Roger smiled at her accidental rhyme, evidence of her terrifying experience.

"Can you do that, Roger? Can you hold me through the night?

I don't promise anything; I just don't want to be alone with visions of pythons dancing in my head."

His answer was found in the gentle way he lifted her from the floor and carried her to his bed where he stayed awake all night, observing her fitful sleep and admiring her exquisite beauty.

Neev awoke with Roger snoring beside her, his arm draped over her. He still wore his khakis, much too warm for the humid climate. Just as she stirred, a quiet knock at the door drew her attention. She moved Roger's arm and looked at the floor before starting toward the door. It looked safe. Peeking out, Neev saw a welcome tray of sliced tropical fruits, little round breads rolled in sugar and a variety of juices in small carafes. What she really wanted, even in the heat, was a good flavored cup of coffee, chilled would even be better. She looked around the room for a table. A small one with two bamboo chairs was located next to the window. The air was alive with calling birds and the pungent aroma of thick foliage in the morning mist. She caught a glimpse of a monkey swinging through the branches just outside the window, and she laughed at its antics.

After setting the tray on the table, she looked for the bathroom. The two rooms shared a bath between them so she could gather her bathroom items and a change of clothes from her own room. The night before, she had not realized they shared the bathroom. Like every other part of the lodge, the bath was austere, a simple shower with a wrap-around curtain, a sink, and a toilet. Bare floors were welcome, cool under her bare feet.

"Well, sleepyhead," she called to Roger as she returned to the room.

"It is your turn to use our shared bath. I'm going to see if I can scare up a cup of coffee, certainly available in the land of coffee beans! I'll be right back. They brought us a tray of fruits. I notice they only put one tray at your door. Someone figured out we were in one room. Our reputation is destroyed! I wonder if the news has spread among our bearers, or if they even care."

"Their imagination will certainly be more active than our

night, hah, unless they can read into my dreams. I wonder the fate of your midnight visitor? You know, the python is not the last of the jungle's surprises. Are you sure you have the stamina for the four weeks we will be shooting? You can still shake hands and return to civilization."

"You won't be so lucky," Neev tossed back at Roger as she disappeared out the door in search of coffee. She did not walk very far before the sought after aroma drew her to an intimate, outdoor breakfast deck, populated with the same Australians from the night before, enjoying steaming cups of coffee on this steaming morning. In the distance, the sun began its climb to the heavens, dew glistening on giant coconut palm fronds.

Working for National Geographic was a labor of love, not wealth. The support for adventures to the unknown gave Roger the escape he needed to chase his orphan blooms. Maybe one day he would make a unique discovery, maybe this trip. Having a beautiful, young woman as a partner might be his good omen. *I wonder what her secrets are, how she became involved in this nomadic and isolated life*, he mused.

"Coffee at last," Neev sighed as she dropped into a chair at a small table, unaware of the admiring glances. She realized she forgot to ask Roger if he wanted one.

"Two cups of coffee, please, with lots of cream and sugar," she ordered from the smiling waiter who seemed to arrive from nowhere and disappeared as unobtrusively.

"I'd like to take them with me." She called after him. Her smile took in the other guests who returned her greeting with the small talk of a new morning full of expectation for adventure. Of course, everyone knew about the snake the evening before. Neev was certain they were laughing at her in spite of their jovial nature.

Neev's unruly, red hair was trapped beneath a beige jungle hat with matching shirt and khaki's covered with the requisite pockets for all the little things that required too much packing and unpacking from a backpack on the trail. High on the list of pocket items were the sprays for bugs and mosquitoes. This time she also had a funnel and tube for those embarrassing moments where she was otherwise not as well-equipped as men to answer nature's call. She glanced at her watch: 6:00 a.m. It seemed everyone was prepared for an early start. The coffee arrived quickly. She picked up the two cups and carried them back to Roger's room, suddenly a little embarrassed at her lack of bravery in the night.

If Neev had read Roger's mind, she would have seen him wrestling with his thoughts from the night before, when she looked vulnerable curled up like a kitten, her sheer, white nightie so revealing he covered her with a sheet, ashamed of himself.

My God, I am old enough to be her father, and I wanted her. I have children of my own. I need to get a grip; this frightened waif just needs my protection even if it is from me.

Nine
Jungle Fever

Roger opened the door wide in response to Neev's gentle tap, greeting her with a waft of Old Spice, a freshly trimmed beard, his thick hair combed, and a mischievous grin filling his narrow face.

"I see you read minds. That's a good sign. Let me at that coffee. I was going to set out on my own quest to see where you disappeared." And the two of them took their cups to the little table and enjoyed their morning meal.

The evening together had prepared them for all the upcoming nights sharing tents and intimate living environments as they traveled along the river and tramped through the jungle brush for patient waits on just the right photo image for the taking. Neev had faith in her own talent; yet, Roger gave her a new perspective.

"Once you think you have the perfect view, take it to the next step. There is always one more stretch to the imagination that takes the photo over the top," he advised her. While she traveled with Roger, she was able to see with new eyes, his at first. Then, she heard herself saying,

"Wait a little longer, go further."

If Neev's friends could only see her now! She was well known for her lack of patience. She waited for nothing or no one. Life was waiting for her, and she was on a dead run to catch up. She was on a run, that is, until she searched for that perfect shot, the perfection of light and subject, the one shot that set her above the rest. She knew it would come someday. Then she would publish her own photo collections, show her work in galleries and maybe return to that land for which she still had dual citizenship. She would send invitations to her mother for her gallery showings. Maybe then, some relative of her father's would see her picture in the press and show up, solving the mystery of her birth and giving her a connection to her roots. She had time for these daydreams, crouched in the deep jungle brush, looking through the lens from the underneath side of the double hibiscus, waiting for the perfect light to reflect off the dewdrops.

Roger was always in contact with the real world via satellite phone, and they traveled with their GPS devices. Neev preferred to stay out of contact as much as possible, to take her mind back to the days before technology, to feel closer to the raw nature around her. She was fascinated with Roger. They had become comfortable with their strange relationship, intimate without intimacy.

They swam in the river naked, waterfalls rushing down the crevices, surrounding them with rainbows and broken pieces of multi-colored shafts of light dancing in the spray, she admiring his taught body that showed no evidence of aging with the exception of a tummy that he fought off with an obsession for sit-ups, morning and night.

Her supple body did not miss his admiration, either. He was torn between protecting her and ravaging her, a battle that wore thin. She made no attempts to make it any easier for him either. He believed she was teasing him, taunting him with her sensual youth, challenging him to reach for her sexuality and take what he really wanted and needed. If he was wrong, and she found him old and repulsive, it would be a long trip.

They photographed each other and timed some photographs that included them both. When he looked at those shots, he saw an old man next to a youthful beauty. When she looked at the pictures, she saw herself as pale and tired and him as tanned and confident. She wanted to experience that body of his making love to her; and their combined thoughts were sufficient for a triple X novel. Her white skin was a constant problem, requiring baths in sun block. Tanning for her meant freckles running together. How she hated those freckles! Using sun block was her only defense. The sun, her enemy. Her breasts and derrière were freckle-free, well almost, in direct relation to which body parts remained most hidden from the sun.

Alas, she died indoors, a slow death of spirit. She required the natural world to thrive. This life was her raison d'être, her passion. She'd gladly add Roger, though. Her fantasies were distracting her from her purpose. Neev caught herself watching him set up for a shoot rather than pursuing her own. She wished for him that he would find that rare flower he was seeking to photograph; but so far, this trip seemed pretty ordinary.

Neev didn't realize he had already found his rare flower in her. He pored over the pictures of her, a radiant smile and brilliant eyes against the jungle backdrop, her white skin framed by that fascinating hair tumbling out of the cap. She told him about her modeling days on one of their long hikes. A beauty was lost from the fashion world to Oxford and the wilds. Roger was the beneficiary.

They grew accustomed to each other, Neev and Roger, generations separating them, but for their common lust after the perfect flower, the magical sunrises and sunsets, the gradients of color from one hour to the next. Their passion for excellence drove them; they were like right hands and left hands, thinking thoughts for each other, catching each other's signals for silence or sound to catch a macaw on the wing, an ibis tracking its insect prey. They caught a chameleon during its color change from brown to green, hugging each other and dancing a jig at their find.

In the few minutes of silence between the day animals hushing with the sunset and night wanderers starting their calls, they would lay on their backs watching the horizon disappear into darkness. Twilight was a wink in the jungle, daylight turning to instant blackness when the sun set without a moon picking up its responsibilities for lighting the darkness. Crossing from day to night became a ritual; and during this brief time Neev and Roger shared bits and pieces of their torn life experiences that drove them to the comfort of an ever-changing, ever-forgiving natural world.

The world of broken dreams and disappointing relationships was far away. Here, even death felt in harmony with the burgeoning life. Roger's parents were no longer living, but he had brothers and sisters that were delighted to have him drop in for a visit and regale them with his tales of wildernesses and deserts, escapes and dangers. He worried that some day he would be a disappointment to them if he came to visit without a tale to tell. He added spice to their lives of children's soccer and an annual trip to Disney World. They all lived in various parts of Florida, his home base as well.

Neev was careful. She always felt awkward trying to tell anyone about her strange life. What acceptable way could she explain a mother so cold that she left her daughter in the care of family friends and strict boarding schools, a mother who refused to tell her anything about her father except that she did not have his name, and he died while she was a baby. Her mother's stubbornness on this issue created the chasm in their already fragile relationship, breaking it completely.

She told Roger that she was adopted by Truse and Rolf in Germany though she was born of American parents. She shared a fairytale youth of being adored and showered with love, all the time feeling odd with the contrast in her appearance and that of her adoptive parents. Her mother gave her an Irish name. Neev's mother never confirmed it for her, but Neev believed that her mother and father had Irish roots because she, herself, looked as though she just stepped off the boat from Ireland. She was shocked when she did travel there to find that the redheaded Irish were actually the recipients of prejudice! Her own mother had dark hair with red highlights that she enhanced with a henna rinse. Neev felt pride in her Irish heritage.

These details she left out in her chats at sunset with Roger.

She told him instead about the little gingerbread town in which she grew up, her relationship with all the shopkeepers who called her their "strawberry angel."

Her German mother entered her in local beauty contests where she rode in floats as the festival queen. She skied cross-country, but never understood the thrill of downhill skiing. Cross country took her into the forests, her camera in her pack, where she could capture the perfect snowflake or little animal peeking out of its winter refuge. She could ski with friends or take off on her own, equally comfortable with her own company in the silence of a snow-laden forest.

As they entered the third week of their sojourn, Roger and Neev started finding each other positively irritating. Neev took too long to gather her equipment in the morning; she dragged on the trails; she lost patience with the timing of the shoots. They argued about the lenses, the lighting, and the subjects. It seemed that nothing could bring back the peels of laughter and intimate moments so enjoyed when their trip began.

Even the terror of the crocs when the tipsy kayak overturned did not pull them together. Roger was just angry with Neev for trying to capture a photo from the unstable craft, turning herself and all her packs into the dangerous river. Instead of comforting her once all was rescued and ashore, he tore into her like a father scolding a child. She was incensed. She had an Irish temper, all right; but over the years, she had learned releasing it gained nothing. She tried to save her outbursts to alone times when she could let loose with words and behaviors that would shock her most intimate friends and family. They had glimpses of her temper as part of her impatience. She seldom let it loose. Until the day the kayak tipped.

"You mean old man, you! There I was floundering around trying to rescue equipment and save the kayak and all you could do was yell at me. I have followed you through this dense jungle, never questioning your judgment in terms of locations or shooting; after all, I am the junior partner, not exercising my own choices

for the perfect photo. We start the day on your schedule; end the
day on your schedule. We take our breaks and eat our meals on
your schedule. When my feet ache and my body is scraped and
scratched along the trail, I continue on until you think the time
is right to make camp and tend to our wounds. Well, this is the
last straw. I don't have dry clothes. You hurried me too fast this
morning. Therefore, you are just going to have to wait while I
wash them, hang them on the bushes to dry, and eat a good meal
dressed in my one piece of dry cloth. I think I saw a small lake
through the trees just before I tipped. I'm going in that direction.
You can follow or you can stay here, mad."

Her loud and angry voice encouraged answering screams from
the birds and monkeys, as she stripped off her wet clothes in front
of him, standing in all her mad fury completely naked, red hair
hanging in long, wet tendrils with the curl released for the moment. She had never been more beautiful in his eyes. She turned
on her heels, wrapping a scarf around her body; but he caught
her by her shoulders, spun her around to face him and pressed
his lips on hers. Her response was more than he had imagined in
his fondest fantasies. The sex was raw and demanding and fast.
There was no intimacy. It was the wild culmination of the desire
that had built for weeks and found its expression through their
anger and the seduction of her youth and beauty and his vitality.
They were protected from the jungle floor by his tangle of clothing and her scarf. They shouted their release to the answering
call of the macaws that seemed to follow them everywhere. It was
dangerous on the ground, their attention on their own sexuality
and not their environment. They dared not linger.

Without words, they gathered up their things and trudged
through the brush, naked, to the small lake she had seen. Fed
by bubbling springs, they found the cool water refreshing and
soothing. They clung together still, uncertain of what happened,
but with full knowledge that it was inevitable. They could laugh
again and enjoy the sensual closeness of their bodies wrapped
together, floating in the water. Her clothes dried in the bushes

under the hot sun, and they had nothing but time. Life at this moment was the perfection of light and subject.

They made camp, dined on nuts and fruits followed with coffee, and spent their ritual saying good night to the day and welcoming the night. This night was not for talking, though. Roger and Neev savored the new step they had taken in the silence of the jungle. Neither wanted to break the mood. Making love that night in no way resembled the fire of the afternoon, but rather the night was spent exploring each other's bodies, massaging aching muscles, and simply enjoying what they had forbidden each other since their first night in the lodge, the intimacy of knowing each other's body and all its sensitive and sensual responses. They communicated with touch all the pent up emotions they hadn't shared. Neither spoke, both fearing that words might end the magic spell. They drifted into soothing sleep and comfortable dreams.

The earth shook them awake while the thunder and lightning ripped across the black sky; stealing the time to savor the night. Their priority was ascertaining that the equipment was fully protected from the torrents of rain. Little rivers came through the tent, but they were prepared with everything hanging from ropes attached to the tent's singular pole. Roger took photos through the opening, capturing the torrents of rain in stills, protected by the yellow water gear and boots waterproofed for the damp jungle. Storms in the jungle were usually brief.

Roger's photographs came before anything. Neev was certain that included her. For the moment, however, she glowed in the richness of their intimate experience together. She had never made love before compared to her night with Roger. She felt alive, aware of her body and the sensual joys possible. She knew he was much too old for her. She was setting herself up for trouble. But at this moment, trouble was exciting. At last her photography was yielding its promise.

When the storm subsided, they started on their trek back to the lodge, part by river and part by trail. They set up for a few more shoots and even a few more pictures of themselves. These pictures were in stark contrast to the earlier versions. The warmth they shared was evident in their eyes, their smile, and the electricity that leaped from one to the other. The lodge was a welcome view in the distance. Both were looking forward to long showers and real meals. The end of the journey was in sight. Where would that leave them? They had traveled from opposite sides of the Atlantic to this rendezvous in Venezuela. What was next for them, either alone or together? Something had changed in the direction of their lives, and neither knew what for certain.

Roger was in an internal, emotional mess. He was angry with himself. This was a young woman who deserved men of her own generation, not a used up old man like him. He had nothing to offer. He had invested poorly and though his income was sufficient for his modest needs, this was a young woman accustomed to the finer things in life. She wasn't going to follow him on his treks, and he couldn't settle into civilian life. He tried that once. His divorce proved it didn't work. Generally, he didn't crave companionship. His passion was photography; his quest gave him his raison d'être. This experience put a whole new dimension in his life that he was ill-prepared to contemplate.

Their same rooms were prepared for them, connecting through the bath. This time, they shared the small shower and found their way back to his bed for glorious sexual intimacy, wild and uninhibited, nothing off-limits. He had long ago made certain he would never father another child. Neither had collected a particularly long list of sexual partners, but they were taking a chance with no protection. It was too late. The unexpected jungle sex had already crossed the safety line. He knew he was safe; she knew the same; but knowing one's own reality doesn't promise the truth from another's. At some point, they had to talk about how far they had come and where they were or were not going.

"Okay, my love," started Neev, already using terms of endearment for this man who had taken her to sensual heights unexplored before. "What is next? Our assignment is only left to the editors now, and any new shoots are up for negotiation. Have you heard what is next for you?"

"No, Neev, my sweet," Roger picked up her tone, "wherever it is, do you think we could form another partnership?"

"I guess it depends on how this shoot turns out in copy. Will our magic be reflected in the photography? We will wait and see. I miss Truse and Rolf. I hope returning to Germany will give us some quality time together. Perhaps you could travel there, too? I would love to have them meet you."

Ah, my Neev. Your adopted family is not going to be thrilled at your old man. You are entitled to a home and family and children. That's what parents want for their own children. I can't take that away from you.

He only said, "Neev, what a great idea. I have some loose ends in Florida, and I will call you. We will take it from there. You call me too. I will have a terrible time leaving your side, but it will make our reunion that much more exciting."

The shoot was phenomenal. The flowers and birds leaped from the pages, and it was one of the most beautiful issues. One of their last pictures together highlighted their partnership in the spread; and the spark between them was evident. It was that chemistry that flowed through the pages they had enjoyed shooting together. Roger was probably right; their meeting was the perfect light and the perfect subject. While the spread was spectacular, he was still short his unique find with the exception of Neev.

They were offered several other contracts together, but none carried the excitement of the first. Their time apart gave them both the space they needed to think logically about what had happened. Instead of lovers, they continued as fast friends and photographic partners. They traveled to Alaska and Canada and Asia, always with two rooms and occasionally what they both labeled, "comfort sex."

Neither found anyone else to fill their nights, but their relationship did not deepen either. They quarreled as often as they laughed. The age difference was telling. They disagreed on just about everything except the regenerative beauty of the landscapes they traveled and photographed. Photography was the glue that held them together.

Ten
Death

That glue was one of the reasons Neev agreed to travel with Roger to Florida, against all her previous resolves about that destination. When he told her she must accompany him without question, she decided she would acquiesce this time, trusting him. Her curiosity was overwhelming. It had been the year from hell for her. They had not spent any time together, although he told her he would rush to her side if she would let him. It was just too late for any comfort. It was too late to fix anything. Death was like that.

After each shoot where they had been partners, Neev always returned to Germany. Rolf died of a sudden heart attack, leaving Truse alone. A strong, German woman with a busy life filled with friends, Truse found comfort in tending the small garden she and Rolf loved. She missed Rolf's strong presence, but she learned to tolerate his absence and was even more grateful for the child fate dropped into their lives. Her arms were a ready refuge for Neev at any time.

She just wished there was some way to tame that roving spirit and give her the peace to enjoy her own home and family some day. Truse longed for the grandchildren that didn't look promising. She knew, though, that Neev had to tame herself before she could spend a lifetime with another person. She had tried desperately to reach Neev with no luck. That was Neev's habit. She would disappear for weeks without communication, returning to Germany with many tales and fantastic photographs.

Truse's face reflected concern, and her tired posture as Neev walked in the door after this particularly long shoot, reminded Neev of that fateful day when Truse told her Rolf was very ill and the prognosis was not positive. Neev's surprise visit was taking a wrong turn.

"What is it Truse? What's wrong?" Neev inquired as the two women embraced.

"Please sit here next to me," Truse said in broken English, even though Neev was raised in Germany and spoke the rich German like a native. For important events, Truse seemed to think Neev needed those events in English.

"Neev, it is your mother. It took some time for anyone to discover that it was she who died in a car crash just outside a small migrant town bordering the Everglades in Florida. She has already been laid to rest and all memorials have long past. You know she sometimes didn't write or call for months, but this time was longer. I should have tried to reach her. A friend of hers sent a box with a few things; there is no estate. I did take a glance inside, Neev, and it is so stark that I was consumed by sadness. I had the joy of you instead of your mother, and now she will never know what a wonderful adult you have become. I did not write to her nearly often enough, thinking that one day you would tell her everything. The box holds a gold baby bracelet with your name engraved, a lock of red hair, pictures of you as you grew up and our address. It just arrived. A sealed letter is also addressed to you. Of course, I did not open it."

Neev felt like she'd been kicked by a horse. Somehow her anger at her mother and their long estrangement had never registered with her as forever. The future always held the fond reunion when they would cry together over their lost years and build a new friendship.

Neev waited too long. She tore up too many of her mother's letters, ignored too many of her emails, returned too many of her gifts. She had been a terrible daughter. Now, she could never redeem herself. Now she was damned. She put away the box without shedding one tear. Apparently, that was, in fact, all that was left of her mother's estate, a woman who lived modestly and died the same. Unknown to Neev, that modesty came from the immense financial sacrifices to ensure Neev had the best life had to offer. Neev's mother lived her dreams on paper. If she could not love Neev, she could at least see that loving people surrounded her and provided the best education available.

Eleven
Once More Before I Die

Fortunately, Neev had the funds and the independence to attend Oxford. The private prep schools were difficult for her mother to finance with the meager school salary. It was okay, though. Her mother's life was just a pretense, a preparation for the next level of existence. The material things of this life had no meaning for the mother without her child. She lived her life in near solitude, other than her days at her work and the heart-wrenching stories she wrote, always hoping for that big break.

Long ago, she lost the passion for living life on the edge, her impatience with life's anomalies and her struggles to have more. She just took each day as it came. "All I know is in this moment," she would say, as though nothing came before or after. She had all the opportunities when she was young. Her life was full, exciting and passionate. What was left was just that, leftovers. She was living beyond her destiny now, one day at a time. She had only one wish that she repeated often, like a mantra, "once more before I die."

She needed to be with him once more. Then, she would tell him. Whenever her life seemed in jeopardy, that thought would come to her. "Once more before I die," she would say in her terrifying moments. In those five words were the cry for the touch that might never come and the story that might not be revealed.

One electric moment validated all that she had become and all that had come before. He reached out to her from the past.

She had just published some short stories on the Internet, and they included her picture and contact information. She had a pen name. No one would connect her passionate short stories with her dull life. An email out of the past stopped her heart, and she broke into a sweat.

"I think you are someone I know quite well," the email said. "If you are that same person, please write back by return mail. Ljt."

The Internet was a wonderful tool for finding lost loves and lost dreams. They had connected once, many years ago, as she pursued her own search for love and career aspirations, and he moved into the corporate world of success. She was certain he filled his life so completely the memory of her was gone. Even the most impassioned memories cooled with time as plans to meet never materialized and she gave up the chance to tell him her secret.

This email stopped her heart. She was tempted to delete it before she thought about an answer. Stirring up old feelings that had nowhere to go was pointless. He made that clear long ago. They were a fantasy, he had explained to her. Their time had passed in his mind; his fascination with her was one where anticipation was the excitement, not the reality.

"Surely, you feel the same?" he asked as they chatted over coffee during a brief meeting at an airport. "We will always be each other's memory of youth and passion, never growing old, never tiring of each other, always passionate in our hearts, untroubled by life's exigencies."

That was not how she felt at all! She planned to tell him the truth that time; but when he took the occasion to tell her about their unlimited fantasy and the impossibility of reality, she lost her courage. He had a life that was complete. She was a fleeting memory that had the intensity of their youthful passion, but was not in the present. She couldn't tell him then. She couldn't tell him just how real their lives had been.

Curiosity was more than she could handle after receiving

the recent email. With a pounding heart, she responded, "Yes, I am here. How are you these days? We have not written in a long time. Many things change. Lm."

That was how they signed their brief touches by electronics, he was "ljt" and she was "lm," the owners of those initials only known to each other.

Those simple words started an email and phone correspondence that sizzled this time. It consumed the spare hours that she used for her short stories, filled her lonely drives in her automobile, validated her passionate side and brought her back to wholeness. Their correspondence breathed life into her soul and awakened her passion.

Meeting was inevitable. They spent days and nights across endless miles of separation, unveiling the many stories of the lives they had not shared. It seemed that "Once more before I die" was chasing them both, driving them to confirm a life-validating connection beyond the present. They both treasured little mementos from their passionate, youthful experience together.

Emails graduated to phone calls; their voices confirmed their desire to spend one more moment together. They shared many life changing events that shaped their graduation from who they were to who they became. Her life was one of change and loss and starting over. His was one of consistency, with his share of personal losses, but a consistent plan. He was a planner. She was impulsive, spontaneous, ruled more by her heart than logic. They were the ying and yang of each other, a split life finding wholeness in their many conversations, revealing that life had not, for all their attempts, returned the prize. His wealth was not the fulfillment he expected; her chase after love left an empty vessel.

With his communication, she blossomed. This new vitality appeared like magic and transformed her essence. Every day was brighter; her dull world became one of excitement. She could share her obsession with the serenity of the Everglades with him. His travels and all their mishaps and tribulations found a new empathy in her. No detail of her everyday existence seemed mundane.

His every description of his world perfected for her the image she held. They provided for each other the missing puzzle pieces to bring them closer with each word. Yet, buried beneath the joy of it all was the anger, the disappointment, the actual hate toward him that she harbored beneath the surface, built out of proportion by the reality of her life without him, the secrets that tore at her very fiber, the dishonesty that colored all the revelations they presently shared.

The little green light glimmered on the chat side of the computer. He was online. She quickly dashed off a note,

"Just had to say hi as it's almost 10 pm for me and I should go to sleep—but will have trouble."

"Ok…I am soooo happy to see your green dots!"

"Me too!!!!"

"It would be a lovely event to find you in the islands at some point…that is the romantic in me."

"Maybe you can take me to the islands; the Bahamas are lovely."

"Did you send the poem you promised?'"

"Yes, I did."

"I read your sexy email with the early departure."

"By the way—did you eat?"

"Not yet…will go put it on the flame now and be right back. I should put some clothes on as I was getting ready to take a shower when I walked into the office to email you and was nude, and never did get back there; so I am still here at my desk working and talking to you in the buff."

"I see you."

"So do my neighbors."

"Then please, dress!"

"Did the verse come through readable?"

"Where? Oh—I did not see the attachment. Going there now."

"Yes. It came through so smooth and touching my heart."

"Good…because I had to wait to send it and would have

preferred you to have had it the next day. It was the only good moments during that last trip! Other than the thong…"

"I don't wish you a second thong, but I do wish you a good trip to me."

He had given her a long tale about a seatmate on his travels whose clothing was more than revealing. They had both enjoyed the sensuality of the story.

"I have that dialed in, and I'm like an Irish setter knowing exactly where you are, will be, and I want to be. I will not stay on tonight as I know it is your sleep time. My dinner is heating, and I will say good night; and I am just dumbfounded that we are finding each other again. Just let me love you is all I ask. I love you, ljt."

"Yes. Dreams of us."

"Good night and sweet dreams of us…and tomorrow. Keep thinking about those clothes you can't figure out yet!"

"Ten to 6 pm, I'll be dressed…although the trench coat is an easy answer—nite."

"Wear it backwards like those hospital gowns."

":-) :-) Loving you with only a few hours left to wait—nite."

"Nite…dinner is ready. Love, jt."

"Kisses and hugs to you."

"You are back, and I'm not gone…and hunger for those kisses and hugs and you…"

":-) I must go to sleep—I'm like a kid before Christmas—really excited…"

"I will sign off and shut down so my pc is not an object you will watch…going away now. I love you. See you in your backyard tomorrow. Loving you, jt."

"I have loved my memory of you for my adult lifetime. Being with you is beyond imagination."

And with those words, she knew, "once more before I die" was a possibility. She nearly went crazy with the thought of seeing him again after so many years of hating him and loving him in a duality of feelings and jumbled memories that kept her psyche in turmoil and kept her from the real joy that life should have been for her.

This time he tried to explain why they parted over three decades ago, why they had been in an embrace one day, and he disappeared the next; why she did not hear from him during her own hellish experience that broke her, that changed her forever.

"I wanted to settle all my own personal affairs before I claimed you," he told her in one of their intimate phone conversations. "Then, when I was ready to find you, you were gone. My letters were returned, 'address unknown.'"

They shared a common thread. Over the many years separating them, they were haunted by their memories and even talked to their ghosts, a fantasy friend with whom they could share intimate thoughts, fears, and hopes that they could voice to no one else. They knew in the deepest recesses of their soul that they had a bond that no time or circumstance could erase. Their recent connection was proof they were correct.

She listened to his explanations, and she was glad to know too late that he had, indeed, loved her with the passion she craved and feared. Their youthful abandonment of reason and uninhibited lovemaking at every opportunity was their expression of their passionate connection that could not be satiated. He was as caught up in their fire as she was; he didn't abandon her. He intended to return. In his absence, she made decisions that separated them forever: permanent decisions that were colored with anger.

So, here they were, meeting again at last, two adults on the verge of retirement, probably grasping at their youthful memories as a last gasp before succumbing to old age. She almost wished it was not real, that they would just continue their fantasy by email and telephone, because reality might spoil it. Perhaps he would be shocked by her age, remembering their youthful vitality and forgetting how long ago that really was. She aged reasonably well, but she was heavier; her face was lined. She joked that there was more sand in the hour glass.

She looked in the mirror and saw her mother, not her vision

of herself. Oh well, in spite of all the sensual talk and words of love, this meeting was just to say hello, to capture a little drop from the fountain of youth. In the big scheme of things, it was not all she was trembling about. It wasn't sufficient to make her heart race and her blood boil, even though that was happening. She knew his physical appearance, youthful or aged, would have no negative impact on her. She loved with her heart, not her eyes. Hopefully, he loved the same way. Hopefully, he would forgive her. Now that she understood the truth, could she tell him the truth as well? Did God give her this one last chance to make amends, to correct a terrible mistake she could not overcome alone?

He called as he drove south to The Palmetto, the hotel where he would stay for the night, the one night they would have to walk on the beach, share a full moon, relive their youthful memories and perhaps hold each other in an embrace that spanned the time apart and healed the wounds of distance. The very intensity of the evening's expectations was terrifying. Perhaps meeting him was the wrong decision; instead, she might let him feel the pain of abandonment, punishment for the aching emptiness of lonely nights and painful loss that she endured. No, they deserved the heaven that belonged to them both. She was ready at last.

Twelve
Good Bye

She spent four hours trying to look younger, thinner, brighter, sexier, and anything else that might have him see her favorably. Her slacks were too tight, but black. Her full breasts were really too much for the deep, rose bustier; but it matched the jacket; and she kept the jacket buttoned a little. She worked the makeup over in the natural light; and her hair was the best it could be, a little too much henna bringing out a brilliant red. It was too late to tone it down; red would be a surprise, but better than gray anyway.

They exchanged a wonderful array of pictures by email. She had been very careful to send the pictures from the past. She didn't have a great collection anyway, not even owning a camera. When she needed pictures, she bought one of those throw away cameras and was done with it. A camera was one more gadget to travel with and worry about losing. She certainly had no talent for it anyway. Mel's talent was the written word, not the visual image. She appreciated an artistic eye, and knew what was great in the talent of others. She admired the artists who touched her soul. She was humbled by their talent.

She saw talent in his photographs. He told her this time that he always had a flair for photography, developing his own black and white photographs as a young man. He had not yet shared with her the pictures he took during the Viet Nam War or his other travels in Europe, Asia and Africa. He did share recent photographs that gave her insight into his present life. They touched her heart. They challenged her thoughts. She loved him even more for the self he poured into the framing of perfection through the lens of his camera. For an amateur, he was an excellent photographer. She suggested he might exploit it more, maybe enter contests. He listened to her suggestions. She was unaware that he filed them away for the future, touched by her interest in this small part of his life.

As she drove into the hotel parking lot, she remembered they had no photographs of the two of them during their youthful courtship. They were always too busy loving to record the events of their relationship. She had one worn picture of him on a ski slope with snow falling. He had a beard and only resembled the young man who stole her heart. She made him pay, more dearly than he would imagine, for that piece of thievery.

The elevator from the garage to the lobby seemed to take an eternity, knowing he was nearly there, her heart racing. Mel bought a couple sandwiches to eat at the beach, as they would have to rush to catch the sunset. She opted for healthy wraps, believing he would prefer that to cold cuts. Paying the bill, she spotted a thin gold, tin box of mints entitled, "oral fixation" to polish off the light, picnic meal. The elegant box was embossed with two slender apparitions, likely a man and a woman, symbolic to her.

With great impatience, she waited. She waited, sitting in the intimate seating area decorated with exquisite orchid plants, a touch of elegance. She had a clear view of the elevator that he would exit from the garage. She would see him before he saw her. She went through her mind whether they would just hold hands, or hug or kiss: decisions; decisions. She was too old for this distress. Shall she run to him like a 40's movie, all the passion pouring fourth and music reaching a crescendo? Or wait, sophisticated and subdued, holding out her hand to a friend?

In the middle of panic, she saw him coming through the hallway in her direction. He wore casual linen slacks, a Hawaiian shirt and boat shoes. Still slender, he was not as tall or broad-shouldered as in her memory. With her weight gain, she felt uncomfortable; but this was not the time to worry about appearances. She walked confidently forward, smiling; and they said "hello" and hugged, lips brushing in a platonic kiss, appropriate for a public lobby. He was obviously uncomfortable, a little nervous, almost like a blind date.

Oh dear, he's sorry that he came. I am not what he expected. Those feelings he thought were forever are for the past, not the present.

"Which way to registration?" All business for the moment, they still held hands as he walked briskly to the desk, registered and departed for his room together. He handed her a room key without comment that she tucked in the purse side pocket. Mel stood by his window, watching the sun disappear on the horizon beyond the bay, while he made a quick change into beach clothes.

If we were still young, I wouldn't be standing at the window. He would rip off my clothing; we'd already be ravaging each other on the bed or even here. We're not sex-crazed anymore. We are civilized, aging adults.

However, she knew she was lying to save herself. Her feelings were, in fact, the same as in her youth. She craved his arms around her, his mouth on hers, his body crushing hers. After the emails and phone conversations that reached a level of heat worthy of self-destruction, their stilted conversations and awkward moments upon meeting were out of touch with that fantasy world. This was reality.

This was not the reality, however, in which intimate secrets were revealed and lives were changed. He was very formal, with little bits of conversation about packing a few things.

"Hurry if you want to catch the sunset on the beach," she encouraged him. The sun was already starting its downward trip and she felt doubtful about the sunset, all her romantic picnic on the beach plans in peril.

"If we're going to act like tourists, the least I can do is provide you with a worthy guide." They hustled off to her car and a quick drive to the beach where the moon rose on the wings of the setting sun that left only a rose glow on tips of wispy clouds now drifting across the rising moon. The bugs at twilight might be ferocious.

He was a brisk walker; she pushed herself to keep pace, her steps matched his own. Without warning, he stopped, pulled her into his arms and kissed her with unexpected passion, the same thrill she remembered rushing through her soul. Without a word, just a tighter hold on her hand, the walk continued.

Was that a test? Was he checking to see if the same chemistry was still there? Well, it was for her. She ignored her response and continued with the planned evening, suggesting, "We can eat there in the beach house or sit on the beach." She carried their supper in a small bag. He had the circular disk that would open to a beach blanket just right for the two of them to have their repast.

"Here is fine!" They tried her romantic picnic. The food was healthy; they split a salad and took bites from their wraps. However, between the mosquitoes and the no-see-ums, the beach walk lost its flavor. They gathered their leftovers and he wrestled with the beach blanket disks until Mel had to rescue him. It had a mind of its own as the wires required magic folds to reduce the blanket to a circle that fit in its container. Their laughter filled the night air and relieved some of the tension. After their short walk on the beach with that one nearly passionate, explorative kiss, they sat for a while on the cement tables near a restaurant, listening to the lapping tide crawling up the shoreline.

He filled in some more blanks from his life, she from hers. A few more puzzle pieces were put in place. He made sure to let her know that he believed "sex is overrated" and took the conversation to a very platonic level. Only the hands that touched reflected the intensity of the emails. This was a meeting of friends, not lovers.

The conversation lagged and he suggested, "Let's return to the hotel. I have a long day tomorrow." The evening was still young.

Disappointment hovered like a thief, stealing hope.

I get it. He didn't find the young, sensuous woman he remembered; instead he found a slightly overweight, aging woman; and his fantasy is blown. He realizes he made a mistake. He can hardly wait to get away.

She was angry. Her "Irish was up." She did not expect a sexual rendezvous in spite of his very suggestive conversations answered with equal verve by her; she did expect a long evening of holding hands and sharing tales of their lives. She did expect their time together to be full of affection: a kiss, a hug, sitting in one of the little nooks in the hotel's lower lounge, snuggled up next to each other in comfort, two old friends with much to tell, her in particular.

Instead, he told her to drop him at the lobby; and the anger she still carried in spite of wanting him more than life itself, found its ugly way to the surface. She was dropping him from her car like a nondescript passenger, saying goodnight from the driver's seat as he departed, feeling a deadening finality that robbed her of the chance to unburden her heart and clear her debt.

"So, this is good-bye then," she said as he stepped out of the passenger side. Sarcasm dripped from her quiet resolve. She wanted to scream at him, to tell him the truth with loud and pulsing anger, to purge her pain once and for all time. Instead, Mel continued in the same monotone as Jack walked to her side of the car,

"Have a nice life, Jack. I have loved you and lost. Thanks for the memories." He opened her door, pulled her out and took her in his arms. Mel stiffened.

"You're angry with me," Jack confirmed in a subdued voice.

"Yes, I am angry. However, do not worry. I will get over it. I will move on. You already have." And with that, he released her and she watched briefly as he walked away.

Mel did not continue watching him leave. If she had followed his departing back longer, she would have seen sadness in his gait, a measure of his distress that she could not have fathomed or understood at that moment. She gave him enough time to clear the entry and stepped on the gas to drive away forever. All the way home, she chided herself about her stupidity. Well, maybe she finally learned. She made all the right decisions after all. The mixed hate and love she bore for him were justified. He was just as selfish as one part of her let her believe, the part that made the ugly choices. She would take those decisions to her grave. He would never know.

She parked her car in the garage at home and rushed to the shower to wash off everything, the sand and salt from the beach, the hairspray, the makeup, his kiss, his touch, his embrace. In the shower, she screamed and cried and shouted all the obscenities she could muster to release the anger and disappointment. She washed it all down the drain. She did some of her best thinking in the shower. Her friends called her, "obsessively clean."

Showers were her balm, whether recovering from illness or heartbreak or physical exercise. Walking in the warm, Florida rain was also a joy. Maybe it was a remnant of her early catechism, baptism by water as a purifying ritual. She would never answer another email from him. He was as dead to her now as he was many years ago. That's the only way to end a love affair, walk away without looking back.

Mel stepped out of the shower, toweled dry, and slipped her naked body between the sheets, satisfied that everything would get back to normal soon. The highs and lows would go away. The beauty of the swamp would give her serenity back. The challenges of her work would occupy her mind. Friends and family were scattered about. She would make a better effort to spend time with them. A trip to Germany was now a necessity that could no longer be ignored. Dumping the emails and the email provider should not be delayed or she might change her mind. She turned the computer on for just a minute. A flash of green shocked her resolve.

"Do you still have the room key, and will you come back?" flashed on the screen.

She was lost.

"Yes." She responded and turned off the computer. She dared not risk looking again or thinking again. She could only act on instinct. Her instincts told her they were not, after all, finished. She threw on sweats, combed back her still-damp hair with its silver threads, packed a few things in a backpack in case they were up all night and she had to leave from the hotel for work. The story she was prepared to reveal might take all night. She made no attempt this time to look any better than who she was. Mel already endured what she believed was his rejection. If he called her back, it was his heart speaking to hers. The exterior did not matter.

Thirteen
The Fog

Mel drove through the fog rolling in from the Gulf in dense clouds that hid the changing colors of the traffic lights. The key Jack handed her at check-in was like a gesture of habit; she really did not think much about it at the time; it was still tucked in the side of her purse. That made it easy. He called her on the cell phone to be sure she was on her way. She thought he might have changed his mind; she thought she might change hers as she followed the winding road through the fog with the tower barely looming ahead. He wanted to be certain she was okay; that she was coming back. She parked in the garage and took the elevator to his floor. She slowly entered the key in the lock, tapping on the door at the same time. He opened it, half dressed. He had a hanger in his hands, putting away his slacks; standing just back from the door's opening in his shirt and socks. Only the bathroom had a light. The room itself was dark except for a little glow from the full moon that challenged the fog.

He said, very quietly, with a tired smile, "Let's go to bed."

There was no sexual intonation, just fatigue. His words were spoken as if "going to bed" was a natural choice for them. Mel wasn't even certain if he meant together or separately as the room offered two queen beds. It did not matter. She had one more chance to unburden her guilt, one more chance to reveal everything. Mel was a little caught off guard but was in his spell. She thought once that he had sexual designs when he suggested they both have HIV tests a few weeks before their planned reunion. She was shocked at first, and then decided to be sophisticated about the whole thing and followed through. Her situation made it a redundant test, but if it gave him less distress, okay. After all, they knew little about each other's adult life and had not shared any concerns about previous partners. She had a couple questionable partners, but had always used protection. He wouldn't understand that. He was the only man with whom she had thrown all caution to the wind. He was the dangerous man in her life.

His trip had been exhausting. Mel felt like they were an old married couple, comfortable with undressing for bed. She brought a conservative sleeping gown. Just to be in the same room with him at all was good enough for her; maybe they would talk through the night. She could take the next day off work if needed. He gave up the bathroom for her. She took her backpack and changed into her sleeping clothes, her heart racing with fear and anticipation, with love and hate. He waited for her, holding the sheet back for her to slip her body in next to his.

"I sleep naked. I hope that's okay with you." Mel knew that. She usually slept naked also; but this occasion seemed to require sleeping clothes on her part, something at least to separate them.

She was mindless, the effect he had on her. Whatever he wanted was okay at this point. She was just plain exhausted. Sleep would be a welcome release from the stress, the emotional roller coaster. Comfort was sufficient. She had on enough clothes for the both of them. Mel snuggled under the covers, feeling his body heat that took her beyond the moment just to be that close again. All the anger disappeared, replaced with pure hunger. Oh, God, how she ached for his touch lying next to him so still, not wanting to disturb his sleep. He seemed so formal compared to her memory of him, so corporate, so civilized, totally unlike the raw, passionate young man who wouldn't take no for an answer in their youth, taking her to his bed with passion and desire that taught her its match. She learned to love him and him alone. She didn't forget, ever. It was her curse.

He reached for her. Mel tried to stay still, but the more he touched her, the more she remembered how it felt to love with abandon. She would never deny him. Never. With her help, he removed her sleeping gown and she forgot the bulging thighs, the tummy and the breasts that were sensual on her younger frame but not the same today, as she fought off the shifting body shape of middle age.

Time stood still and then raced backward. She was young again, and so was he. They were lost to the fire of their youth, now the fountain of youth. His body was still hard and muscular and excited her every sensuous place he found and loved and touched until the ecstasy came again and again as he took her beyond any expectation at their advancing years. Oh, how grateful she was that her body yielded to him, all the sweetness that was for him alone, all the sounds she muffled in the pillow, wishing they were at sea so she could scream her ecstasy to the universe. It was his love that gave her life; it was his alone that filled her soul. Until this night, Mel was a shell of the woman who loved him in her youth and never loved with the same passion again.

He, too, found his moments of release; and somewhere around three in the morning was certain they were satiated for this moment in time. They shared smiles and anger; he wondered why she didn't say no to the intimacies she had refused in their youth. She said she was following his lead; she was only going where he wanted to take her. Mel was his as much this night as the first time he took her to ecstasy. If she denied him anything then, she could deny nothing now. She wanted to be as he remembered and bring nothing new to their lovemaking. Even so, she wasn't as shy as then. She wanted to be even more assertive but held back. They congratulated each other for the chemistry that time had not erased and the bodies that fulfilled their desires.

They moved to the second bed to attempt a few hours sleep after a quick shower, their bodies wet with sweat and lovemaking. She would have stepped in the shower with him, but was suddenly conscious of her aging body now that her mind was returning from its release to pure joy to the present moment. All that conversation she had planned did not come to pass. Mel lay against his back, trying to be still again and allow him to sleep. She didn't sleep much these days, but he had told her in many night conversations that he needed a full night's rest. He certainly wasn't getting one tonight, and he had a long day's drive ahead of him.

The cell phone alarm chirped its morning message. He suggested she use the bathroom first, and she was quick. He was anxious to leave, to get on the road. The urgency to leave filled the air. They almost ran from the room, but he stopped for a coffee for them in the lobby. As much as she adored him, she had the feeling still that he was sorry. In the garage, they parted with a hug worthy of good-bye forever, each entering their own car and driving to the end of the lane and then turning in opposite directions. She felt him moving away from her, her own body feeling the pull as the full moon takes the tide away from the shore. Mel felt wonderful and terrible at the same time. Wasn't that the truth, though, of their entire relationship? She was reminded of the game she played as a child with flowers, "he loves me; he loves me not."

She knew he loved her; but he also did not want to love her. She haunted him as he haunted her, but they made choices; and their choices kept them apart. His choices kept them apart now.

That night was their last. He told her in their many emails before their meeting that he would never leave her again. It was a promise he could not keep. There were a few emails afterward, but they never carried the passion that preceded that fateful night; and they became shorter and less intimate and revealed little about hearts and souls and more about the exigencies of daily life that were destined to keep them apart forever. Bit by bit, their touch by email became a pitiful "Hello" at best. He still called now and then. They might talk about her stories or his photography. Mel still wanted his touch, craved it more than before; but it was her yearning alone to bear. He was done. The calls stopped along with the emails. The silence was a loud and clear message that needed no interpretation.

Mel continued her life as though this event had not occurred; yet, there was a piece of her still crying, "once more before I die," because there was still unfinished business. She thought fondly of the green lights on the computer greeting each other, reminding her of lightning bugs that flash at each other until they find their true love, and mate. When he left her this time, reality set in destroying the fantasy that had lingered before. It was easier to walk away from reality. Facing reality took courage. She was an expert at walking away. She wore that path quite thin. Perhaps their night of passion was imagined, not real after all.

Fourteen
Roger

Roger grew weary of Neev's pouting bouts and little temper bursts. Her impatience was wearing. At first he passed it off to her Irish inheritance and her youth. He still chased the perfect photo shoot, but he accepted fewer assignments. Neev was angered by his lack of interest, she who needed the excitement of new adventures and challenges at every turn. She began accepting assignments of her own. Their initial passion disintegrated to a comfortable on-again, off-again friendship and partnership. When they did travel together, their work product was still unquestionably more captivating than either produced separately. He was losing his status as her mentor and lover.

Their different interests seemed to separate them also. Instead of looking for common threads to follow, their choices took them in new directions. Neev liked the flowers and small animals; but she also liked the large, wild animal kingdom. She spent weeks in South Africa on Safari getting much too close to the wild animals to "see into their eyes" she would say as Roger shuddered at her reckless endangerment of her own life and those who traveled with her. He was most comfortable in the swamps of Louisiana and the Everglades of Florida. She refused to travel there. At first, because she knew her mother lived somewhere near the Everglades; and she would be bound to make amends. Eventually, she refused on principle.

Roger was disappointed when Neev would not accept his comfort during the grief from her mother's death. In their long friendship, she finally revealed the complexities of her youth. He wanted to go to her in Germany. He wanted to travel to where her mother lived and see if he could get more information. Neev forbade him from participating in this part of her life. She threatened to never see him again. He remembered how that Irish anger of hers had broken the relationship with her mother. He didn't want to take a chance.

Her refusal to accept his comfort hurt a place deep in his heart; that place where trusting the one you love builds the deepest bonds. He knew Neev was making sure that distance remained between them. She wouldn't let him touch her soul, only her body, and that was seldom anymore. She told him a friend of her mother's had sent her a box with pictures and a letter, but she had locked them away without looking; and she doubted she would ever look at them again. This chapter of her life entitled, "parents" was closed forever. She would never know the truth about her father; she would never have a chance to find resolution for the hatred between her and her mother. As was her habit, moving on was the best medicine.

Not long after the news about her mother's accident, Neev traveled to South Africa for the Safari shoot. The National Geographic photographers and staff members were like a small community. Everyone passed each other along the way in the most remote places in the world. A rumor reached Roger that Neev was involved with a safari guide. He wrote it off to grief and immediately forgave her in his heart. It still stung. She was young and entitled. He was worried, though, that she lacked the capacity to love in a lasting and committed way. Love required trust, and Neev did not trust anyone. She said that was why she loved the animals. No one expected her to trust them. She judged them by their known instincts and behaviors, and they seldom disappointed her.

Roger received an assignment that he decided would interest Neev and perhaps help them both. He was assigned a photographic documentary about the Roman ruins and their impending decay from aging and tourist abuse. It was a chance to enjoy Europe and work at the same time. Perhaps he would at last get a chance to meet Neev's family in Germany. At least she would be close to her home and with him.

A year passed since her mother's death; the Safari was behind them. He wasn't getting any younger and needed to take some of these more pleasant assignments. Neev promised to meet him in Rome, and he made the arrangements for them. He traveled first to Florida to visit with his own relatives. His life of travel had worn out his body a bit. He felt it in his bones, moving a little slower and trying special diets to fend off the arthritis. He had a hunger for roots, comfort in his old age.

Roger's brother lived on a small, developed island on the Gulf Coast of Florida. Roger's family labeled him the "flower child" because of his obsession with flowers in all parts of the world. Roger accepted the nickname with good humor, even sharing it with others occasionally.

Thus, it came as no surprise when his brother told him he ought to set up his cameras at a nearby Audubon Society sanctuary and capture some of the wildlife there in addition to exquisite swamp hibiscus and lilies. The purple morning glories also spread across a controlled burn area. The Everglades bounty of subjects was unlimited and one of his favorite locations. He preferred what he called the "true Everglades" deep into the swamplands, reachable only by airboat and hidden trails, tromping through the wetlands of snakes and alligators. He would, however, give this little sanctuary a visit to please his brother. After a day of chasing around with his nieces and nephews, a day for photographs was a very good idea. It was a hot July day, but his own experience with the Everglades told him it would be cooler in the sanctuary.

He arrived in the morning and chatted with the guides before setting out with his camera. While they were talking at the desk in the cool, main building, another, excited guide came rushing through the double glass doors.

Fifteen
The Ghost

"You'll never believe it! This tourist is looking for owls in the canopy above the boardwalk and spotted a white, ghost orchid. I'm not kidding! I looked through his camera lens and there it is in all its exquisite beauty, dancing in the breeze, laughing at us all! He didn't even know the magnitude of his discovery!"

The guide's excitement spread through the little group, and Roger's excitement exceeded them all. He already participated on quests through the Fakahatchee Strand, suffering ticks and hostile walking conditions in search of just one ghost orchid bloom. These orchids were exceptionally rare, and orchid collectors from all over the world traveled to their few sightings just to view these rare finds. Their natural habitat was Southwest Florida and Cuba. They were high on the endangered flower list with large fines and potential incarceration for anyone who attempted to remove one. Maybe his chance had come at last; maybe his perfect light and perfect subject might be found in photographing this rare orchid.

Roger reached the location on the boardwalk just as the tourist was tearing down his own equipment, but the blooms were barely visible in the distance with the naked eye. "How was your photo session?" Roger asked.

"I think quite well. However, I see you have more specialized lenses. I'm just an amateur, but I have taken quite a few nature and landscape pictures. My next lens will be more like yours," he responded in a quiet, almost subdued voice.

"You look familiar. This is one of those strange days for me anyway, my first time in a swamp since I was a young child in Louisiana. I hardly remember those days."

"If I seem familiar, it might be because of National Geographic. I'm Roger Andrew. My family calls me the 'flower child' because of my obsession with rare blooms at rare moments anywhere I can find them.

"Sometimes, a news reporter is interested in my work; and a flash sends my face across a news wire. Normally, the ghost orchid would cause that kind of a stir in the press. I don't think I've ever heard of one so clearly visible by the naked eye so high in a tree, so easily seen from a public walk. The guides said none has ever bloomed in this sanctuary." The two men with only an orchid in common exchanged business cards and continued the conversation while Roger set his camera just right and waited for the clouds to pass the sun so the lighting would improve.

"How did you happen to come all this way to this little sanctuary?" Roger continued after he glanced at the little business card and its California address.

The tourist thought for a moment and then answered thoughtfully, "I had a friend who lived near here that encouraged me with my photo endeavors. I retired recently and just had the time to travel a little further for some special photographs. My time share company opened a new resort about forty minutes from here, so I took the leap and came for a vacation and the chance to discover nature in its primeval best. I might even say I was compelled. Finding the ghost orchid on my first quest in the Everglades has been an experience that will haunt me the rest of my life. Do you know how often they bloom?"

Roger's knowledge of the ghost orchid was limited, but he knew from past experience that they bloomed in their own time, sometimes dormant for years. Attempts to grow them from seed were often unproductive due to their fragile nature. This uncertainty was part of what made them so rare, in addition to their fickle nature, their delicacy, and their stark lack of green foliage.

Roger shared that information with his new colleague whose equipment was packed and ready for departure.

"Thanks for the extra information. I'll keep your card. If my pictures turn out reasonably well, I'll send them to you. I'll watch your web site for yours."

Before the two men parted company, they shook hands, smiling. Roger felt as though he, too, had met this man before. Something about the eyes and that smile filling the narrow face drew his attention. Even the tall, thin frame walking away with purpose through the swamp felt familiar. Whew, he was getting spooked by the rare orchid find himself. He didn't have long to think as the rest of the guides and the sanctuary staff arrived to set up the scope and label the site. Roger took a few more pictures and vowed to return.

The next day, the newspapers declared that this rare orchid had appeared from nowhere, high in the crotch of an ancient cypress tree, as rare in its appearance as in its endangered status. First, a ghost orchid had never bloomed in this sanctuary before. Second, one had never bloomed or ever been discovered anywhere in the world this high in a tree. Third, any ghost orchid blooms that had been previously found were the result of quests deep into inhospitable swamps. Fourth, the number of blooms, eight at one point, was astounding. Those on a quest were lucky to see one. They were so rare that thieves were an issue with this discovery. Security cameras were installed around the site with volunteers staying with the viewing scope.

This was the first ghost orchid visible to the naked eye from a public boardwalk. Each bloom was worth thousands in the open market; and so far, the count was nearly eight blooms that would remain the swamp's treasure alone. Roger cut out the article and put it in his camera bag. He returned several days at several different times to take photographs, hoping for that perfect shot. He was often inconvenienced by the roadwork. New turn lanes were being paved and marked for the entrance to the swamp. Shiny new guardrails followed the curve before the entry. Bright, orange cones lined the road, and flagmen directed traffic around the new tar and the new markings. He noted that this turn was probably dangerous on this curve before the changes were made to the road. In fact, the changes did not entirely eliminate the danger. His inconvenience was small compared to the safety benefits derived from the improvements.

Roger packed away his orchid pictures and their story to attack at another time and caught his flights that took him to meet Neev in Rome. He looked forward to their first shoot together since her mother's death, the African Safari and Roger's trip to Florida. He expected many challenges. However, he missed Neev beyond comprehension and hoped she was anxious to spend time with him also.

Sixteen
The New Adventure

Their former, easy camaraderie was missing. Neev and Roger felt less free and more restrained. They stayed in their separate rooms at a cozy inn not far from the Vatican and didn't talk about anything significant beyond their contract and the difference in photographing inanimate objects without a life force compared to living flora and fauna. Neev insisted, "Even the ancient ruins have an aura, a mystical quality that gives them a life of their own."

Roger said their only choice for photographs was the changing light and time of day, the shadows and the shapes. No life existed in the ruins for Roger as he thought, *just like no life remains in our relationship.*

Roger drove their little rented Smart Car with the same abandon of traffic signals and rules as any other Italian. Neev spent most of her time as a passenger, terrified and buried beneath the camera gear. "Please, Roger, let me drive," she pleaded to no avail as they took one holiday in the country, driving to Sorrento for the beauty of the coast and a quick ferry ride to Capri. As luck would have it, they missed the last ferry and had to be satisfied with their walk through the old city and with the trinkets purchased from little storefront vendors. Neev looked with longing at the train before their winding and mountainous trip back to Rome in the Smart Car.

Roger tried to tell her about the ghost orchid adventure, but it touched him deeper than he realized and was too deep to share with this distant young woman, this stranger that used to be his Neev.

He checked his email upon returning to the hotel room, late in the evening. Surprisingly, there was a brief message from his new acquaintance from the ghost orchid sighting. "The ghost orchid is blooming again. They never bloom twice in such a short time span. I lost a small camera bag strap at the sanctuary and called the office to have them send it to me if found. The guide told me about the second blooming. I guess that's pretty amazing. I thought you might be in the area and want more pictures. I've attached my best one. I'm adding it to a Coffee Table book I'm self-publishing just to share with friends and relatives and for my own enjoyment. The second blooming is more spectacular than the first, eleven blooms this time, a record. It should last another two weeks or so. I saw your shots at your web site. Congratulations; they are magnificent."

Roger opened the attached picture and was surprised at the professional quality. He could almost see the graceful ghosts dancing in the swamp breeze, long slender tendrils dropping from delicate blooms springing into the air, barely attached to the tree crotch, no leaves or readily visible roots, just a close look revealing the roots wrapped around the tree, a blend of browns and deep greens. The light gave the petals a sheer, gossamer effect. For an instant, an image of Neev flashed across his mind, that first evening in the jungle lodge, her sheer, white nightdress barely covering her slender body as she shivered, frightened, in the center of the bed. The image was only fleeting, and Roger felt a little silly.

Of course, he could hear Neev in their connecting room, knowing that door would remain shut. She filled his thoughts anyway. Associating her with the orchid was the natural result from her occupying every little empty space in his mind when they were so close yet so far from each other. How had they lost their connection? Was there anything he could do to bring it back? Maybe they should just sever their partnership so they could both move on. He was no longer good for her. She had her own contracts now, her talent equaling and exceeding his. Oh, she still looked to him for advice occasionally, but he believed she was patronizing him. He was becoming an old man, and she was still in the flower of her youth.

Two weeks. That was how long the orchid was expected to bloom the second time around. However, this ghost orchid was far from typical. Roger had flown half way around the world before on a quest to capture the perfect shot. Why not once more? And why not take Neev?

"Neev!" Roger knocked on the connecting door, and eventually she opened it.

"Okay, you got me out of bed. This had better be good!" She was in one of the many foul moods that seemed to consume her lately. It didn't have any impact on her beauty. Even in anger, she generated a sensuality that was unequaled in Roger's experience. He wondered if something had gone really badly with the Safari, either the rumored affair or the shoot itself. Or was it the death of her mother that brought out this angry, almost sullen disposition. Any other time, opening the door would have brought a smile at least, a greeting of affection, even if intimacy didn't follow.

"A tourist I met at the sanctuary in Florida, you know, the ghost orchid shoot when I stayed with my brother; well, the tourist is an amateur photographer who took pictures also and sent me one. His email says he's going to publish it in a Coffee Table book for his family and friends. I like the idea. You and I should have thought about that, not for our family but for our financial wellbeing! Anyway, what do you think of the picture?"

Roger opened the door just wide enough for Neev to see the computer screen. She wore a conservative, deep green, satin lounging suit. As she moved through the door with her eyes on the screen, she felt the orchid reaching for her, pulling her closer, to see the image clearly. A chill slid up her back as Neev stepped into Roger's room to examine the photograph with her professional eye.

She had to admit, it was beautiful. It captured a rare, haunting beauty, stark yet compelling. The light was perfect, revealing the sheer, gossamer petals and a hint of the slightest movement, not stopped completely by the shutter, as the tendrils danced below the branch. To her it looked as though the dancing blooms were trying to fly away from their roots, still attached to the tree's trunk. She was amazed at the poignancy of the picture, of the many stories it seemed to tell, almost like a painting. She looked from the perspective of its photographer, to feel his fascination, while she tied it to her own emotional response.

"Okay, Roger, what's the catch? I'm not sure why we're so impressed by a photo for a Coffee Table book. Care to clue me in?" Her mischievous nature broke free as her hazel eyes brightened, and one of her recently rare grins spread across her face.

"We've finished the ruins. I want to travel to Florida and catch the second blooming. I think you'll enjoy it also," he suggested.

"You've been trying to get me to travel to Florida for years. I didn't go when I should have; I'm not going now when it's too late." Her angry outburst was instant, but Roger ignored her and continued.

"Then, do this for me. I'm starting to tire of the travel, but I still hope for that one last shot at perfection. I have the feeling this might be it. Too many coincidences tell me not to ignore my instincts. First, I was at the sanctuary on the day the first bloom was discovered. Neev, this orchid is a rare and endangered species, seldom found so easily or so accessible. It never blooms so high in the canopy or with so many blooms. But now, it bloomed a second time with more dancing ghosts than when it was first discovered. This is extraordinary beyond imagination. And there's more. You have to look at the orchid through the scope or the camera's lens and watch it dancing in the breeze to feel its power. It's almost mystical. You and your Irish roots should be able to appreciate mysticism. I feel its pull. I don't want to go back alone. Just come with me on this one last shoot, not because you want to this time, but because I want you with me. I want to share this experience with you."

This was not like Roger. Neev was the impulsive one. Not only was she impatient with waiting for anything, she wasn't much of a planner, either. Just as she jumped from modeling to Oxford and Oxford to National Geographic on whims, her travels were often unplanned. She really needed Roger to plan for her. Yet, in her photography, her patience was infinite for the perfect shot. Her instincts were as nearly perfect. She could wait for hours for just the right breeze to move a leaf or light to create the needed shadow. That was one reason why she was such a fascinating creature; she was unpredictable. She might agree to travel with him for friendship's sake even if she abhorred the idea, or she might refuse altogether. The silence seemed eternal before she carefully crafted her answer.

"Okay. I'll go with you to Florida. I don't want to, but we have a long history of caring about each other; and I haven't been much of a friend lately. I am sorry for that. I think I have taken my own personal grief and turned it to anger toward you. I do not know why, only that you are the closest person to me other than Truse. Truse is getting too old for me to carry my burdens to her. I don't want to burden you. Therefore, I am just plain angry; and you are the recipient. If traveling with you to Florida will make it up to you, let's go. Let's go right now before I change my mind."

Roger did not give Neev the chance to change her mind. They packed that night and took the first flight out of Rome to New York with a connection to Southwest Florida International. The Kia Sportage was ready for them at the airport. Roger made reservations at the most elegant hotel on the west coast that was within any reasonable driving distance to the Everglades. Their swan song would be worthy of their history if his planning worked its magic. He knew this was the time he had to let her go.

Seventeen
The Message

A short distance north of the turn into the swamp, the driver of a little red sports car lost patience with the dump truck ambling down the two-lane road, in spite of the double yellow line around the curve. As he sped into the oncoming lane to pass, the driver in a white, foreign sedan completed her left turn directly into his path.

The passing red car was hidden by the slow dump truck. It seemed there was plenty of time for the sedan's left turn. The red car raced past the truck and into view as she turned. Her desperate attempt to avoid the head-on collision with a terrified spin of the steering wheel sent her sedan careening toward the ditch, "once more before I die" flashing through her thoughts as she saw her beautiful swamp spinning upside down just before impact and darkness.

The next day, after the crumpled vehicles and broken body were taken away with screaming sirens and helicopter blades kicking up whirling dervishes, young boys were riding their ATV's along the road.

"Hey, there's a cell phone," one called to the other.

He stooped over and picked it up where it lay glinting in the sun, hidden in the brush. It was in perfect condition! He clicked the text messages. The last and only message was at precisely 1:20 p.m. the day before, "I love you and miss you. I will call later. ☺."

The ditch was torn up, with glass everywhere and a few remnants from the wreck still scattered across the fields and shoulder. "I wonder if this is from the accident. What do you suppose I should do with it?"

"Let's take it to the Sheriff; it's no good to us anyway."

The sheriff's office found no information in the cell phone that would shed further light on the accident. The phone number for the text message was blocked without a trace. No other incoming calls, outgoing calls or contacts were saved. It was one of those go-phones without traces, without documentation.

The memorials ended, and the woman who traveled to this community to work was just one more casualty on a dangerous, two-lane road. Someone erected a cross and wrapped it with purple plastic morning glories in the tradition the community had for marking the spot where a loved one's spirit spent its last moments. It was quite a while before the guides at the swamp mentioned that they had not seen their friend recently.

"Oh, didn't you know?" one guide shared with another. "She died in that terrible accident at the entrance. I read the newspaper article and even saw the photographs, but it was some time before I realized she was the same woman who walked here every day. She loved this swamp so much; I hope her spirit finds its way back."

Eighteen
The Tourist

A year passed. Jack's retirement trauma was long gone and he settled into a life of golf, tennis, home and hearth. His behavior gave no clues that something terrible had happened; daily life was in the perfect pattern he planned when retirement was on his horizon. He certainly didn't miss the travel. He actually wore it out of his system during the last few years of reporting to work. Yes, life was good to him. His health was generally exceptional, although he suffered bouts of anxiety that seemed to increase in their intensity recently, interrupting his sleep pattern; usually a good round of golf provided a healthy escape.

Home was his sanctuary. He enjoyed telling stories about the wildlife that came into his yard from the preserve that bordered his property line. The deer ate the budding new trees, especially a large buck with a full rack that was determined to remain a pet in spite of his efforts to the contrary. Wild turkeys ran by his office window. Little chickadees almost landed on his outstretched arms. A hummingbird seemed determined to live in his metal storage shed. Once, he was certain he stared down a mountain lion. His love told him about "snake away" to create the perimeter that snakes avoided.

He finally bought a kayak and found hidden streams in the valley where he didn't have to drive quite as far to find the serenity that only a man alone—or a woman alone—on the water can enjoy. She loved kayaking as well, accustomed to rivers that ran downhill but settling for lazy southern streams and marshes where alligators nested along the shore and sometimes noticed her when she disturbed their reverie. She told him about those trips down her rivers, how she wished she had the courage to kayak under the full moon. He thought he would call her sometime from his kayak to hers, but that was before. Sometimes he envied her then. She kayaked to the Gulf in the summer, 90-degree water in salt flats shared with great blue herons and delicate white egrets.

His face was no longer clean-shaven. He grew the beard they talked about. Even though it was gray, it hid the deep lines in his face now that he could barely keep out of the sun as he pursued his activities to maintain good health. He still kept it neatly trimmed. His precisely cut gray hair was definitely thinning when he was seen without a cap, which was not very often. His collection of special caps provided a balm against advancing age, the culprit that he could not stop from stealing his hair and with that thievery, the viral young man he remembered. His arms and shoulders had strengthened with the kayaking, his legs with the mountain bike; his fitness level was at its peak for a man of his age. He walked tall and proud, the same as when he was younger, his slender frame chiseled from his activities and an occasional visit to the gym.

The time he spent with his camera, however, became his favorite pastime, photographing everything from snow in the boughs of his own maturing trees in the mountain foothills to the beauty that surrounded him wherever he traveled. He was collecting some of the best shots, still considering where they might be submitted for recognition. She told him once that he had an eye, that he should enter his photos in a contest.

"You enter one for me," he suggested then. There wasn't time. She encouraged him to pursue art whether writing, painting or photography to explore the depth of his soul where their hearts intertwined. Here he was, camera in hand, preparing for his semi-annual vacation at timeshares he owned, haunted by his memories.

"Photographs from many of my favorite places are already in my collection," he explained to his family, as preparations were underway for a new timeshare destination he chose with care.

Trips to his vacation time share properties had actually grown stale, the same locations year after year. He wanted to start using his weeks to trade for new experiences. This time, he wanted to photograph the Everglades. It didn't really make sense to anyone else; but he was the organizer, the one who made the arrangements; and the trips were always satisfying. This time he selected a new island resort, a sister to timeshares he owned already.

The island was everything he expected, and more. She'd written about the same island in one of her stories where young lovers frolicked in the warm surf and laughed at the antics of pelicans on a fishing pier. Everything felt familiar to him, seen through her eyes. His little band of extended family members were as excited as he was to experience the hot Gulf in summer, the white, powder beaches, the catamarans just off the shore. Yes, he made a good choice after all. This was truly one of the most beautiful beaches in the world. Exquisite seashells lined the shore, pulverized by the pounding surf to create the powdery beach.

In fact, the beach was such a favorite he was given the freedom to travel off the island by himself with his camera and his quest for new subjects. He'd planned his destination for a long time. The news clippings remained carefully tucked away in his camera case since he first received them. No one cared about his camera paraphernalia. That was strictly his domain, just like his locked gun case where he kept journals in a false back.

The date was etched in his mind as deeply as a carving on stone that would never disappear; he was a day off from wishing her a happy birthday in spite of their good-bye. The least he could do was call her on her birthday, he thought. He didn't leave her because he loved her any less, but because he loved her too much. Their bonds just had to be broken by one of them, and he was the one who did it. He was sorry for the pain, but the break was necessary; without it, neither was able to move on completely. Their connection was always part of their existence. At least he convinced himself at the time that a final break was the right decision. Later, he knew better.

At precisely 1:20 p.m. that fateful day, when he knew she would be finished with her walk through the swamp, he sent a text message to let her know he would be calling. He wanted to be certain she would answer. He had a block on his phone number so it didn't show on the screen. He was discreet in that way. Later, when he did not reach her on the cell phone, he felt his essence draining away, just as she had often described the times when he had left her. This time it was a feeling unlike any he experienced before, filling him with anxiety.

Desperation to reach his love drove him to call her repeatedly to no avail at home and at work or anywhere over a twenty-four hour period of time. Perhaps she was still angry. Maybe he misjudged her strength in adversity. Maybe this was one more painful experience too many. He promised to love her forever this time, to never leave her; and he left anyway. He called the number she gave him as an emergency contact and reached her distraught friend. She had also called until she was the recipient of terrible news; they cried together over the phone. She sent him the newspaper version by email to the account he had shared with his love alone, the email account he still could not bear to close, that just sat there in cyberspace as empty as that place in his heart.

He ignored the information about the memorial and the burial and anything else that was sent to him email. Eventually, the emails stopped. The line in the newspaper article that referred to the cell phone text message at precisely 1:20 p.m., the time of her death, left him wondering whether he had distracted her and caused the accident. This fear built in his psyche until it seeped into his sleep and deepened the anxiety he bore in addition to his silent grief. No phone number was traced. Witnesses only saw her pull in front of the truck and the passing red car; and it happened so fast, it was a blur. The truck driver survived, oblivious to what had occurred. She died in spite of the Herculean rescue

effort with helicopters and hospitals. The driver of the red car survived thanks to Mel's swerve to the ditch where her sedan flipped
into the air and landed upside down. His life was spared from a
head-on crash while her quick swerve caused her own death.

Mel told Jack about her beloved swamp where she walked
every day. It was her salvation from the job in the impoverished
Everglades community where her talents seemed wasted. Sometimes, though, she suggested there must be a higher purpose for
her role in that community. The swamp was her sanctuary where
her communion with nature was even deeper than what he felt
in his own home environment. He tried to fathom the depth of
her connection to the unique environment she described. The
last story published under her pen name tried to capture some
of those emotions.

The bridge from the island to the mainland crossed over ce-
rulean seas below with endless blue/gray heavens above, white
puffs of cloud drifting by, fishermen along the sides dropping
their lines in the receding tidal pools. He drove off the island toward the sanctuary, leaving the busy and divided highways for
the two-lane road she had often described as dangerous. After
nearly an hour, he finally reached the gate. The turn lanes appeared newly tarred and painted; some bright, orange cones were
still around, dark tar defining the improvements, marked with
clean, white lines for turning lanes. A cross across the road from
the gate with sun faded, plastic, purple morning glories wrapped
around it caught his eye.

My God, had someone put this up to honor her? The faded and
dusty tribute did not escape him, providing no comfort at all.

He remembered her description of the parking lot where she
parked in the shade of a tree at the end because the sun was blaz-
ing hot on the car by the time she returned from her walk. He
believed he found the same tree. He gathered his camera equipment, hat and water bottle and approached the building she often described. There, behind the desk, sat an elderly gentleman
with white hair, a mustache to match, and a southern accent. Was

this the man she talked to every day? He paid his twelve dollars and started a lonely walk through her cathedral. The canopy protected him from the burning heat of the sun though the air was hot and humid.

He stopped in wonder as the curving walk led to an open marsh where bright yellow flowers crowded each other, racing for the sun that spilled its golden essence as far as the eye could see. As he looked to the left and the right and straight ahead, the spindly cypress trees were but sticks at the edge of the vast sea of gold. He was not certain whether the sun had poured molten gold across the marsh or whether a rainbow had dropped a golden ribbon. Those were the only stories that could adequately describe the view. She sent him a picture once, but it did not capture this excitement, including the sweet floral aroma wafting across the boardwalk.

Nineteen
Who?

The boardwalk led into the cypress forest where he looked up to the heavens as she described her very own walks, listening to the sounds of the wisp of wind through the cypress trees, the occasional deep-throated bark of the alligators, one woodpecker calling to another and even the familiar sound of an owl calling, "Whooooo?"

Who? Who was it that called him here? He knew. He felt her haunting presence all year, pulling him toward this swamp that meant so much to her. Vivid dreams broke his sleep and caused him to awake in a sweat, her hand across his chest, her lips brushing his cheek.

Feeling her presence in the swamp was so compelling that it eased the anxiety he felt from his belief that he contributed to her accident, that he was the reason her laughter no longer echoed through the cell phone; her little sarcastic barbs no longer pierced his heart. The ache in his loins would never again be satisfied by the love that poured from her heart to his.

She walked beside him in this place. She once said this was where she wanted her ashes thrown to the wind to find their way through the cycle of life that pulsed through the Everglades. He did not know what happened after the accident or whether those wishes were honored; what he realized though was her spirit hovered around him everywhere in this place, in the air he breathed, the mist rising from the fern-shrouded floor, the breeze; and he believed she forgave him for leaving her; that she was smiling at him for trying to find the serenity she promised him from her swamp.

He set up his camera a couple of times to take pictures, first of the blood red leaves that appeared as a large bloom on slender stems and then the white lilies. He saw why someone might wind the cross with purple morning glories. They bloomed everywhere, large purple cups on vines that spread their tendrils across the charred remains from controlled burns or lightning strikes. Squirrels and chameleons danced across the boardwalk, teasing him to take their pictures. Giant grasshoppers in full dress colors also joined the parade. Butterflies darted from flower to flower, following him.

The heat was nearly unbearable, pushing the envelope to nearly one hundred degrees. Except for her presence, he was quite alone. He was not accustomed to the humidity; it weighed heavily on his chest. It seemed as if he was walking in a rain forest, the humidity hanging in drops from the trees and the broadleafed alligator plants, mixed among the giant ferns, reaching for the sky. The soil was dry. Only a few cardinals darted here and there. A woodpecker or two bobbed their red heads, drumming for dinner. A hawk screamed as it sailed across the sky; and he looked high, the sun glinting through the trees. Perhaps he'd also see one of her owl friends.

Overhead, the sun caught glistening tendrils from a delicate white flower high in the crotch of an old cypress, its green roots wrapped tightly around the tree's large trunk. He saw rare orchids in Hawaii; the sight of an orchid was not unusual for him. However, he'd seen no other orchids anywhere on his walk to this point. It was difficult to see clearly, the sun in his eyes; but he was certain there were several blooms. He decided to focus his camera equipment toward the orchid to see better and perhaps catch a picture in the unusual effects of the sun's light on the dew swept flowers high above the boardwalk. He set his tripod.

A guide stopped to see what he was capturing in his photograph. "Oh, it's just an unusual flower, a white orchid I believe.

Actually, I counted eight blooms, I think, high in the crotch of that cypress. Here, take a look for yourself. How many do you count? Some may be wrapping around to the back of the trunk."

The guide's excitement surprised him. He was not prepared for such a stir. "That is a ghost orchid," whispered the guide in a husky voice, as if releasing his real excitement might scare it away. "It is rare and on the endangered list. It has never appeared in this sanctuary before. This is a mystery of immense proportions. Maybe it came as a seed or cutting on the winds of a hurricane, blown here from a distant location. They are found elsewhere in the Everglades, but seldom so visible. People go on quests deep into the swamp just to get a glimpse of what we are seeing just off this path."

The guide looked through the camera; Jack looked with his naked eye. The tendrils hung from the delicate, ethereal blooms, almost gossamer in texture, and moved gently in a breeze that seemed to wind its way through the swamp, an eerie breeze that pulled the humid mist along with it, giving him a chill in spite of the day's humid heat. When the guide stepped away from the camera, Jack took a picture, knowing full well that he could not capture the feeling that was wrapping itself around him.

"Would you mind leaving your camera in place until I bring the other guides from the main building to set up a viewing station? We'll set up a scope so every visitor to the boardwalk will be able to see the ghost orchid."

"Sure." He was in no hurry to leave. The guide told him that this was, indeed, a miracle. It needed to be shared with others lucky enough to visit the swamp on this day. People traveled from all over the world on quests to find ghost orchids deep in the swamp, often missing their bloom, the timing so very delicate, as delicate as their exquisite nature. For some, the love affair with the ghost orchid was matched by no other flower; the quest for its beauty became an obsession. A book and a movie cataloged one man's obsession, and the book's author followed his trail through the unforgiving swamps without ever seeing an actual bloom, only experiencing the misery faced by intruders into this very unique universe. Yes, he was led to this miracle. This was, indeed, a day to remember.

He was a very practical man. He didn't believe in ghosts or spiritual messengers or likely even angels. He was uncertain about the spiritual side of life and had his own questions about his own mortality. The prospect of his own death caused him no fear, but he didn't like the uncertainty of its claim or the untimely way in which it snatched away the woman who filled his heart and whose absence left the void she so often described in her own soul.

As he admired the beautiful, white ghost orchid, a sense of calm settled in to replace the anxiety he experienced since feeling the life force drain from him nearly a year ago. It was as if that life force was filling him again. The more he stared at the flower and its dance in the swamp breeze, the more serenity claimed his being. He was almost afraid to glance away until he saw the man with the camera approaching, followed in the distance by several men and women dressed in khakis carrying viewing equipment stands and signs in their hands.

He enjoyed his conversation with the photographer. They agreed to exchange photographs, sharing business cards in the meantime. The man nearly looked through him, saying he felt they had met before; there was something so familiar. They laughed at that and shook hands. The photographer remained at the site while Jack walked away, dropping the business card carelessly in his pocket. The photographer watched the parting back, still caught in the feeling of recognition…even to the proud walk.

Jack let them take over his spot. He had his picture. He listened to the hoarse whispers behind him about the history and tales associated with ghost orchids.

"You know, they are often associated with graves," said one seemingly knowledgeable guide.

"Yes, but whose grave is high in the tree, there?" came the reasonable reply.

Jack knew. He knew why he was compelled this year to follow her call to the swamp. Whether her ashes found their way to the soil was irrelevant; her spirit found its way to its home. She was here, all around him, telling him she forgave him. It wasn't his fault. She was where she belonged, floating in the breeze, watching over her beloved swamp, in all her unique beauty and delicate soul. He was right about one thing. Her strength was not in meeting adversity; she experienced the pain with deep grief. In that, he had not been kind. Her strength was in loving him unconditionally, even as she sent her spirit to take away his anxiety and set him free.

Not too far from the setup for the orchid's viewing was a bench. He remembered she told him about her favorite place to sit and listen to him on the cell phone, whispering back the replies. Cell phones were actually forbidden on the boardwalk, but this was where they shared some of their most intimate thoughts. He threw away the phone he used to talk with her when he learned of her death. He smashed it to smithereens in his pain and anger that she was taken from him, that he did not have the chance to tell her he was coming back, that he would never leave her again. He was sorry. He was not a prince, their secret code based on a little book they both enjoyed, but was just an ordinary man from whom her demands for intimacy taxed his ability to give; but he would try. He would try with all his heart to deserve that unfailing love she had so often professed and that he had equally spurned.

Today, he knew she understood. Her untimely death was for some other reason than a distraction from his call. The love she bore for him was everywhere around him in the whisper of the breeze, the beauty of the ghost orchid, the flowers he had already photographed, and even the chill of her spirit enveloping him. "Thank you, my love," he whispered, and he was at peace.

He rose at last, gathered his equipment and walked back toward the ghost orchid. Would it still be dancing in the breeze high above the canopy, overlooking her domain? A guide stood sentinel at the scope and told him the photographer had gone after more equipment. It wasn't quite the same as when he was alone with his own camera. Yes, even through the scope, the flowers remained as compelling as the first sighting. No, he would not return here again. This place belonged to her. With her fond good bye, he was now an intruder. His life and his destiny were no longer tied to hers; she had truly set him free.

The rest of the walk along the boardwalk had few distractions. He felt like running with joy except it was not appropriate. He wanted to develop his photographs. He was anxious to return to the resort. The drive back provided just the right amount of time to contemplate his experience and put it in perspective. He was ready to leave it behind as he pulled into the hotel parking lot. There was still plenty of beach time left for long walks to think about all that had occurred on this strange journey.

He developed the photographs immediately upon returning home. None were as captivating as the ghost orchid. It almost came alive from the print. He enlarged the best shot and framed it, giving it a place of honor in his study where the beauty of the preserve spread out beyond the windows. He brought the beauty of her swamp to meet the beauty of his preserve and knew she had a hand in it, and all was well. At last, all was well.

He kept his word and sent an email of his best photo to the photographer he met in the swamp. He had some unexpected news to share as well. He realized a small camera strap was missing and decided to call the swamp in case he had lost it there. The guide was more than helpful. He told him the ghost orchid had bloomed again, almost exactly thirty days after the first blooming. This time, there were at least ten and possibly eleven blooms.

This news was unnerving at first. While the guard shared the information, Jack's hand clutched at his chest where he felt his heart racing, as if his hand could slow its rapid beat. Was this another message? Was she calling him back again? This time, he couldn't answer her call. The best he could do was carry out one of her suggestions and publish some pictures. He was putting together a Coffee Table book that would have the ghost orchid on its cover, a tribute to her. He sent Roger the message that the orchid had bloomed a second time. He looked at his own ghost orchid photograph. Was she looking back at him? Did she still have more to say?

Twenty
Déjà Vu

Neev insisted on driving. Roger's sight was not what it had been. He neglected to tell her he was developing cataracts that were not yet ready for removal, one of the reasons he needed to cut down on his travel. Hopefully, once he had the surgery, his sight would return to normal. The road to the sanctuary was a two-lane, winding, dangerous road with dump trucks passing each other and nowhere to turn. The shoulder-less road edge led to deep drainage ditches where beautiful birds fed among the flotsam. The contrast was noticeable, beauty and filth side by side. She also thought she saw a dark log with eyes, likely an alligator, in the ditch.

They drove toward the sanctuary from the north, an easy right turn to the access road. The new markings were finished; and the big, orange cones were gone. Roger felt something great was about to happen as they drove the winding path to the main building. His anticipation built. Good reasons drew him back to this rare bloom, including his insistence that Neev accompany him. For the first time, he noticed the cross at the entrance wrapped in purple plastic morning glories, faded from the sun. He found the habit of marking accidents gruesome. The turn into the swamp was dangerous before the changes, coming off the blind curve.

The guides greeted him like an old friend; he introduced Neev. The older man with the gray mustache and the ready grin did a double-take when Neev smiled at him. Roger just saw the usual magic, the way men of all ages responded to that electric smile and those penetrating eyes. The guide saw a familiar face, a face that had smiled at him nearly every day. Of course, it was coincidental. There was no need to bring up a terrible accident and the resemblance. It would only seem morbid.

"Welcome. I hope you enjoy your time here. You have come on a special day as you can see by all the pictures of the ghost orchid on display. Our little treasure has bloomed a second time, this time with more blooms than before! Do look at the rest of the pictures in the store. Some lovely note cards might make a nice memento. This is a once in a lifetime experience."

"We are here for just that reason," responded Neev, catching the excitement. "Roger, here, thinks this may be the picture we have spent a lifetime and world tour chasing. What do you think?"

She smiled to herself as she thought about her famous partner, obviously unknown to this guide who was so proud of the pictures in the room. They were lovely, but they lacked soul.

"You cannot go wrong, miss, if the light is right. There's a bit of cloud today, but hopefully it slips away until you have your pictures. The scope is up so you shouldn't have any trouble finding the location."

"So this is the swamp you love so much. Your precious Everglades." Roger expected a sarcastic remark to follow and was surprised, "Well, Roger, once again, you are right."

As they reached the marsh just before the official swampland, thousands of miniature gold and white flowers replaced the purple morning glories, spreading a brush of gold and silver from the edge of the first trees, across the marsh, and to the edge of the cypress forest. They swayed in the breeze on spindly stems that were barely seen beneath the profusion of gold and white. Neev took in a breath of their beauty and smelled the pungent aroma.

"Oh, Roger, this is amazing! I want to run through the flowers and have you capture my ecstasy with your magic camera!"

But of course, they remained on the boardwalk, following the rules. The photo opportunities were endless. A few morning glories still bloomed near the ground. Tall stalks of wheat-like plants, similar to sea oats, danced above the goldenrod and wild daisies, their silks shining in the sunlight. Butterflies, every color and design, chased from bloom to bloom. It was a photographer's paradise. Neev held out her hand and one almost landed on her fingers, brushing her skin with a tiny puff of breeze from its fluttering wings. At that moment, a flash of light reminded her of Roger's expertise. She hoped his photograph captured the magic.

Step by step, walking deeper into the thick brush and cypress, surrounded by the calling birds and gators, wading birds in the pools on either side of the boardwalk, Neev's lifelong anger started to dissipate. "Whoooooo?" startled her to a dead stop, and she was eye to eye with a barrel owl. She laughed, that gleeful, child-like laugh Roger had not heard in a long time. The woodpeckers still beat their chorus, red heads bobbing high above. Neev was having a wonderful time, almost skipping ahead of him.

Roger spotted the scope. They had it to themselves. As they approached the part of the boardwalk just before the ancient cypress with the ghost orchid's roots wrapped tightly around the trunk, the cool breeze he remembered from his last visit provided a brief relief from the still heat. He looked at Neev to see if she noticed. She had just touched her arms with her hands, crossing her chest, an automatic response to the change in temperature. It was only a moment. It heralded the approaching location of the ghost orchid. Coincidence?

"Here, Neev, look in the scope first, and then try to see it with your naked eye. I may need you to help me adjust the lenses as I take pictures. I'll get mine set up first, while you look through."

Looking through the scope, Neev was struck with the naked beauty. No picture yet revealed the mystical qualities that filled her view. The clouds lifted and the sunlight reflected off miniscule dewdrops on the blooms themselves, the long tendrils dancing in the one breeze in the entire swamp. The light shone through the gossamer petals, framing them and emphasizing their fragile form. More than the earlier blooms photographed by Roger and his friend, these reached out even further from the tree, ready to take flight and leave their roots behind. Neev felt their pressure to be free. Were they ghosts or dancers? The difference was difficult to discern. In either case, they exuded a powerful life force that reached out to her, just as others felt it before her and would feel it after. The mystery of this unusual flower caught her interest and fancy. She was anxious to set up her cameras and impatient to begin shooting.

The two old friends spent the day photographing the orchid from every angle. Roger was obsessed. He was certain this was his winning photo, his swan song; just as this trip was likely the last that he and Neev would take together. After the time passed for the park's closing, the guides told them to leave. The only shot not yet taken was in a full moon, yet five days away. They had enough for one long day, and they unwillingly tore down their equipment. Neev lagged behind as Roger led the way back to the main building. Actually, she felt something pulling her back, whispering, telling her to stay awhile. She shivered and caught up to Roger, trying to put her free hand in his though burdened with the heavy and bulky photography equipment.

"I think the orchid called to me," she whispered.

He looked at his very pragmatic friend with wonder. She was serious, and she was frightened. He squeezed her hand.

"Remember, I am your protector. I always promised that nothing will harm you when we are together, at least nothing physical. Certainly, I can protect you from ghosts in a swamp. If they are here, they must be kindly ghosts. There is something profound about the orchid, but certainly not to be feared. Hang on tight. We'll be back at The Palmetto in no time."

"The first time I saw the ghost orchid it reminded me of you on our first stay at the lodge in Venezuela, you in your sheer, white nightgown, curled up in the middle of your bed, staring down that python. No, have no fear about the orchid. Whatever whispers you heard were meant to comfort not frighten. Its magic has reached you as well. I hope you have forgiven me now for bringing you here."

"Oh Roger, I am so sorry I give you so much trouble. This day was a purge that carried away the pain and anger I have nourished for so many lost years. Perhaps now is the right time to finally let it go; perhaps it is more than coincidental. Maybe any beautiful place might have the same effect. Timing is everything.

"From the moment I walked onto that boardwalk my senses were bombarded with pleasure and sensations of wellness. I felt the cycle of life pulsing through the trees, in the earth and in the sounds. Signs of birth and life and death are everywhere, mixing together in a beautiful harmony. If I could write a song, I would call it, 'The Swamp Song.' I'll bet even your arthritis has improved."

"What do you mean, my arthritis? What do you know about that? It was my secret." He was also hearing her "swamp song" and thinking, "swan song," the ending of a beautiful era in his own life that was a struggle in hers.

"Yes, Roger, your secret, just as I have no secrets from you. Tonight, I will tell you the rest of my stories that I have held from you, not because you are my love but because you are my best friend in the world, and you deserve the truth. First, I will tell you my name's origins. I'll start that now, on our way to the hotel."

"Just be careful as you turn left out of that entrance. It's still dangerous."

Roger felt a sense of déjà vu as they rounded the corner, turning north on the winding, two-lane road back to the hotel.

"Okay, you can begin."

He had never asked again for her to tell him about her name, not since the first time at the jungle lodge where the question disappeared into thin air. Through all the years that passed, she still remembered the question.

Twenty-One
Heaven

"I am truly Irish, as you often tease me. It is the one thing my mother told me about my father, the only thing. She said she gave me an Irish name that described how she felt in his arms when I was conceived, "heaven." The real spelling is, "Niamh," but pronounced Neev in English. I represent my mother's heaven about which she never revealed another word, and took her knowledge of my father and my roots to her death. I no longer resent her for that.

"I hated my mother for too much of my life, and hers. I want to believe she had a very good reason for leaving me with Truse and Rolf. They gave me a wonderful childhood, so it was a gift. I did not tell you about a box Truse received for me after my mother's death. It contained a gold baby bracelet, a lock of red hair, some pictures and a letter I brought with me to Rome. I haven't read the letter yet. The bracelet has little gold links and is quite delicate, obviously a love gift, inscribed with my name in Irish."

They parked the Sportage and took the elevator to their rooms, spent from the day in the swamp. Neev crawled into bed with Roger, and they held each other through the night. Something wonderful occurred in the swamp, but neither could describe it. A life force wafted through their hearts and filled them once again with love and forgiveness, freeing them from anger and misunderstanding. No, Neev and Roger were no longer lovers but they found a deeper understanding, a connection that was deeper than their first sexual encounter; it transcended sex.

They trusted each other with their most intimate secrets. Nothing is more profound.

The temptation to return to the swamp the next morning was ignored. Instead, they sat under the colorful market umbrellas on the marble patio where they were protected from the Florida sun. Exquisite, Romanesque waterfalls in pools on either side were soothing to the spirit. Neev opened her mother's letter. She knew when she first received the box that she could not be alone with the letter. She did not know it was Roger whose company would free her to understand its meaning.

"Thank you, Roger, for being here. I'll start reading it, and see what it's all about." Neev opened the envelope carefully and began to read out loud to Roger.

"Dearest Neev. If you are reading this letter, I am no longer here to watch over you and steer the course of your life. My own anger and grief kept me from answering many questions for you. I was selfish. I can never make up to you for that selfishness and only hope your discovery of the truth is not too late for your life to be enriched. Before you continue reading this letter, you may wish to read the pages I have saved for you from my journal."

A few loose-leaf papers fell to the table, pages torn from a journal or diary. They were numbered in different color ink than that in which they were written.

"I guess I should read these loose pages first."

"What am I to do? I am certain I am pregnant. How can it be anything else? We made love day and night, barely stopping for the necessities of life. How I love that man! He filled me with the joy of life through the ecstasy of his touch. So, the child of that experience is at least a child of love. The fact that I am in no position to give birth to a child is secondary. No one must know. He's gone. We had a clear understanding that ours was a short-term experience, that when he left, it would be forever. We didn't count on a child. If I tell him, he might come back. But if he doesn't, can I live with that? I'm torn between love and fear."

Roger was still paying close attention as Neev continued to

read, "I have a solution. I will try to keep from showing as long as possible and then visit Truse and Rolf. They have been begging me to visit. Perhaps they can offer suggestions for my dilemma. They helped Emma when she was pregnant; they will know what to do. I can disguise my situation as a visit to friends that is long overdue."

Neev interrupted her reading to explain a little more about her foster parents to Roger.

"In Truse's youth, she backpacked with friends through Europe. She met my mother and Rolf in a youth hostel, and a deep and lasting friendship was formed. They continued their backpacking together, Truse, Rolf, Mother and another friend, Emma. Unknown to her traveling companions, Emma was already pregnant before the trip began. When they arrived in Germany, Truse knew a good doctor and the pregnancy was terminated. She and Rolf were older than Mother and Emma, welcome protectors.

"Truse and Rolf became inseparable and rented a small apartment together; Emma and Mother stayed with them until Emma could travel again. On a dare, Truse and Rolf married; their new friends and old friends celebrated the nuptials together, celebrating for weeks afterward. Over the years, Mother and Truse continued visiting each other and corresponding. Truse and Rolf always wanted children, but it didn't happen for them."

"I'm starting to understand a little more about your life, Neev; please continue."

"Okay, I'll continue with Mother's journal pages,

"Truse and Rolf are thrilled at my impending visit, whatever the reason. I'll keep my secret as long as I can and then depart for Germany. I have no other choice. I've just been too busy to write lately. I'm sticking to a diet quite well and am, luckily, experiencing no nausea or symptoms. I still ride the Jeep to work every day and feel quite well."

Neev picked up one more lose piece of paper and continued,

"Well, I can't hide my condition much longer. I think I'm

six months along. I've made the arrangements to visit Truse and Rolf. I took a leave of absence and can return to my teaching if I wish. It will be a relief not to worry about appearances. Rolf and Truse will help me. They are dears."

Roger picked up the pieces of paper and put them back in order as Neev started to read the last loose piece, "Today is my seventh month. Truse and Rolf have been wonderful, insisting I stay with them until the baby is born and as long as I need help. What will I do then? How can I show up from an extended visit abroad with a newborn child? What shall I do?"

Neev returned to the letter. She did not see the compassion in Roger's eyes as she read, yet, she felt his comforting presence.

"You were anxious to be born. The pains came suddenly. I'd barely told Truse and Rolf before they were calling in the midwife for an anxious delivery. You were born two months early, barely breathing and frighteningly tiny.

"I was deathly ill; an infection set in immediately. I was delirious much of the time. Truse devoted herself to my care and to giving you a tender start in life. You were born bald, but soon bright red hair—the color of copper—covered your tiny head. I looked at your sweet little face and I saw the man who came and complicated my life and disappeared. Every time I looked into your eyes, I saw him and the bitterness rose in me like bile.

"Depression settled in like a black cloud. I could do nothing but cry. I didn't want to hold or care for you. I was afraid. I left your care in Truse's capable hands. Truse was a natural mother.

"No medicine made any difference. I was either crying or angry; I wasted away to under a hundred pounds. I didn't want to eat or sleep or get out of bed. I fantasized that death would be a welcome release. Truse became frustrated that she could find no way to bring me peace or share the joy of my beautiful child. Finally, with no argument from me, they committed me to a clinic in Bad Nauheim."

Neev paused and wondered if she should continue reading this very personal account to Roger; maybe it was too much information. He looked at her with such understanding that she continued. He was, after all, her best friend.

"My refusal to share information with them about the father so they could go to him for help was another cause of distress to my wonderful friends. I said I would never reveal his name unless he came to me of his own choosing, loving me and wanting me. Otherwise, I would carry my secret to my grave. At the time, though ill, I kept my promise. I never intended for that decision to be a wedge that divided you and me for a lifetime. He was dead to me, and that was the story I would tell you.

"My illness detached me from the normal love a mother has for her newborn child. Today, the medical term is post-partum depression. I was incapable of caring for you, and Truse and Rolf willingly took on my responsibility. I did my best by naming you "Niamh," a good Irish name that you have always known meant, "Heaven." I also made sure over the years that you understood you were a child of love even though it disintegrated to hate. Your father and I came from strong Irish roots, and I believed a strong Irish name would give your tiny body the strength I lost. I was in heaven when you were conceived, regardless of how it turned out. Yes, Heaven is the right name for you. I hope you can forgive me someday for the rest of the story."

A tear escaped as Neev struggled to continue reading, "After the clinic declared me well, I left for the United States. I sent a long letter to Truse and Rolf giving them a power of attorney to take care for your necessities of life. I believed you would only be with Truse and Rolf a short time until I was settled and could figure out a way to bring you into my world.

"Truse and Rolf were already dreading the day they would have to part with you. They were as attached as if you were their own child. What kind of mother would leave her child behind in a foreign country and return to the United States? I was an unfit person, much less a fit parent. I was still too filled with anger and loss. I determined to see you often and claim you back when I could. Maybe your father would find me and we could claim our daughter together. Over time, I realized that thought was only a fantasy."

Neev's sobs interrupted her reading, bringing Roger's strong arms around her.

"Stop reading for now, Neev. Let's walk for a while and let this news sink in a little."

"My father might be alive!" Neev exclaimed. "My mother said he was dead. Truse and Rolf only repeated that she refused to tell them anything. I might not be an orphan after all. Roger, I must find him. I really must. Surely someone who knew my mother also knew my father! Maybe there are more papers somewhere, more of my mother's things that I don't have. I wonder what happened to her computer. I was in such shock at her death that I never inquired about anything. Now, I must know."

"Let's leave it alone for now," consoled Roger. He had not seen her so agitated before, and he was worried.

"Let's walk in the garden and talk about this mystery that has begun to unfold. Maybe Truse has something of your mother's that might help us plan a strategy. So, Neev, my sweet 'heaven'. I could have told you the meaning of your name. You certainly brought a touch of heaven into my life."

They strolled in the gardens, her arm linked through his, their walk slow and thoughtful. The lush, tropical foliage with fountains and lagoons crossed by bridges and walkways were the balm needed. They wandered along the paths for twenty minutes or so, each in deep thought. Neev's tears dried at last.

Twenty-Two
The Puzzle

Roger was generally not a puzzle person, but he was wrestling with pieces that seemed to be falling into a place that aroused his curiosity. If he was right, he might have something special to share with his Neev; if wrong, he might give her hope for nothing. However, coincidences were far too many for none of them to fit. He decided to keep his thoughts for another day and wait for her to read the rest of her mother's letter.

After dinner, they settled into the settee in Neev's room where she continued reading,

"I tried desperately to figure a way to bring you back into my life. At a minimum, I sent as much money as possible to Truse and Rolf. They asked for nothing, but I didn't want them to forget I was your mother. If I spent money to travel to you, I would have less to send for your care. Eventually, they didn't encourage me to come, either. Perhaps it was better not to have the confusion of two mothers. Truse was wonderful about sending pictures and updates.

"So many years passed without you that I hardly believed you were part of my life. There were years when I tried to live a normal life. You were this beautiful child with carrot red hair and snapping hazel eyes in some dream world where I did not participate. I asked Truse if I should send pictures of me, or write letters to you. She advised against the idea. I sent letters anyway, pictures too; but you didn't write back. I decided it was too much to expect from a small child. I did send you a camera as a gift, hoping you would send me pictures. If I wasn't going to be your mother, it was better if I just left things alone. There was no question you were showered with love and caring.

"You had your fifth birthday before Truse told you about me. It was no wonder I never heard from you. I planned a trip to Germany then to give you the camera myself. Truse said you were inconsolable, and it was better if I didn't visit that year. It seemed all I could do was cause grief. Life is cruel. Every day you looked more like your father. I hated that part of you. I couldn't help it. I saw his eyes in yours, his smile on your lips. You grew tall and slender, just as he looked when we met.

"It seemed boarding schools were the best possible approach to giving you a solid start in life. The cost was atrocious. As you know, your vacations were too short and precious to take you away from Truse and Rolf. When we had a moment together, we were always quarreling. When I saw you walk the runway in Los Angeles, I saw your father in your face and your bearing. It was impossible for us not to quarrel again when you insisted on knowing more about him. How could I tell you the truth when I lied for so many years? You would only hate me more.

"So, my darling Neev, I have in death a gift for you I could not give in life. Through the miracle of the Internet, he and I found each other once more; I was going to tell him the truth and unite us all at last. I learned much too late that harboring hate is a cancer that eats at the soul and sours the mind. It is too late for me, but not for you. Please find it in your heart to forgive me my transgression and hopefully you will have a chance to know your father.

"I never had an address for him; and from what I know about his life, you may be disappointed if you do find him. He has a full life and his own family. You might be an unwelcome interloper. I have to give you the chance to find out on your own. I have an email address for him that's on the small card in this letter. I also entrusted some information to Truse that she was not to reveal. She may share it with you now. I have nothing else to leave you. I hope your roots give you the peace you need. Love, your mother."

This time, Neev shed no tears. She stared into space and held the email address in her shaking hands as if it were a rare gemstone. It was. She had never truly loved anyone beyond Truse and Rolf…except Roger, and he was more a father figure than the love of her life. She had never really trusted anyone, going through life on a dead run to the next adventure, escaping any feelings that might well up. She always knew a critical piece of her life was missing, and now it might be within reach.

Here she was with the answer in her hands. At long last she had the key to the door that would unlock the mystery man who destroyed her mother's life, her relationship with her mother and her own serenity. Was that an answer she really wanted to pursue? Maybe some questions were there for the asking, but should remain unanswered. At least now she understood the turmoil that governed her mother's life. She understood her mother's anger. And she forgave everything.

What she couldn't understand still was why her father didn't look for her if he knew. Did he know? Her mother's letter wasn't perfectly clear.

Roger gave her the silence she needed, just setting back and watching the anger drain from Neev's face, replaced with an appearance of calm that he had never witnessed. Neev was never calm. He always believed she remained so pencil thin because she burned the calories sitting still, ready to pounce. She was like a cat, watching for its prey. Because of her impatience, he was awed by her ability to concentrate on a photo shoot, the one time she became an entirely different person, controlled by her desire, like his, for the perfect light and the perfect subject.

Neev finally broke the silence. "I need to go home to Truse before I make any more decisions. What is your next plan?"

"I may go back to the swamp and take a few more shots before the ghost orchid blooms are gone. I'll visit my brother. Maybe I'll call my ex-wife and look up my son and daughter.

It's been a long time. Maybe they, too, have found forgiveness in their hearts. I'm feeling old, Neev. You are right, the arthritis is bothering me; and I do need surgery on my eyes. I might even retire from the Geographic and try publishing a few things on my own. You do know, I am always here for you, just an email or cell phone call away."

"Yes, I know. You are my dearest friend in the world, Roger. I am sorry again that it can't be more. You gave me your eyes to find the photo that is one step beyond the first thought, to reach for the perfect light and the perfect subject. Neither of us has found it yet, but maybe we are close. Take care of yourself. I'll be fine with Truse. I'll let you know what happens from there. Thank you for sharing my letter and my gift. I will always remember these few days as our song, our melody for the love we share."

Neev and Roger packed their equipment, their suitcases and their separate challenges of self-discovery and left for their own piece of the globe, Roger for an island off the coast of Florida, Neev for Germany. She put her little card and her precious letter in her purse.

Surprising Truse was always fun for Neev. This time was a surprise, all right. Neev was surprised at Truse's failing health. Truse was her cheery self in any regard and the two shared tears as Neev revealed bits and pieces from her mother's letter. Truse had her own guilt to purge. She had clung to Neev, herself, making only feeble attempts to reunite her with her mother. She had not given Neev many of her mother's letters and gifts. Her excuse was Neev's delicate disposition, the confusion of two mothers. The reality was her fear that Neev would leave. She won; but in the end, it was an empty victory. Yet, she saw no blame in Neev's loving eyes. Neev was overwhelmed with the revelations that built, one by one.

"Yes, my darling. I do have a few more things for you. Your mother always carried one picture of your father. He probably doesn't look like that today, but let me find it for you."

Truse left the room and returned with a worn picture of a

bearded young man, standing in the snow. What Neev saw, how-ever, were her own penetrating eyes staring back at her. Even with the beard, she saw the smile that graced the black and white modeling pictures that still hung on Truse's walls. No question remained in her mind; this was her father. Her youthful fanta-sies were not far from the truth. Truse also had a necklace with a pendant.

"Your mother was wearing this necklace when you were born. I put it in a safe place. She was ill after your birth, and you were quite a challenge. You were so tiny then, Neev. You were born too soon and took a lot of care. Look at you now! Anyway, the necklace was forgotten. Your mother would certainly want you to have it. I think it's a Celtic Cross."

Neev did not share with Truse that she was in possession of the details of her birth. She only revealed the information about her father. Truse's age was showing; the remaining years they had should be filled with joy, not a history that might create a rift between them. Regardless of the pain Neev experienced, Truse and Rolf could not have loved their own child more. She held them faultless.

Neev told Truse about the email address, though. They de-cided together that perhaps the best thing would be to let the news settle a little and then possibly send a careful email. After so many years, he would be an older man and might not care to know he had fathered a child he had never known. Neev needed to think about the shock and whether she really wanted to re-veal herself at this late date. Perhaps knowing he existed, know-ing the truth, was sufficient. Perhaps the truth alone was the gift to which she was entitled. She fastened the necklace around her neck and felt closer to her mother. The necklace must have been important.

Twenty-Three
The Perfect Subject and the Perfect Light

"Ghost orchid blooms for the third time," read the caption on the picture, tucked away in the local section of the newspaper. Roger was one of those people that read the entire paper, discovering the little articles missed by the masses.

Roger could not believe it! How could he be so lucky? The article in the local paper was small but went on to say that this time was not as glorious as the last two. Only two fragile blooms were visible; how long they would last was questionable. They bloomed at the right time for him to notice. He was very busy since Neev left for Germany. He was on a quest not much different than his search for rare and endangered species; it was still detective work.

He returned to the swamp and spoke with the guard who seemed so taken with Neev. The guard told him about an attractive middle-age woman who visited the swamp during her lunch hour for many years until the fateful day of the accident that occurred before the new turn lanes at the sanctuary entrance were completed. He said he almost mentioned the resemblance between that woman and Neev but didn't want to seem morbid when Roger and Neev looked so happy about their adventure. After all, it was only a resemblance and certainly nothing worth bringing up to strangers.

Roger found the news article about the accident in the archives of the local newspaper and drove to the school where she worked. With great effort and charm, he pried a little information from the young and disinterested secretary who guarded the sign out log as though it was sacred. His instincts were correct. Neev's mother walked the boardwalk daily at the very same swamp where the ghost orchid bloomed.

The accident occurred where the swamp entrance met the highway on her return trip to work, the dangerous left turn. She never made it back on that fateful day. Instead, she died alone in a local hospital, had a memorial sparsely attended, and nothing more was known. The first ghost orchid bloomed about a year later.

The secretary told Roger that a few things were sent to an address found at her home, but her possessions were few and unremarkable. Her life was pretty much a mystery at her school. She did not talk about anything personal and her demeanor kept anyone from asking. She worked quietly and efficiently, keeping to herself, apparently biding her time until she reached retirement.

The ghost orchid was no longer a coincidence, he knew. He knew he was called to this swamp to experience the ghost orchid: Neev was the reason. Somehow, he had to share his discoveries with Neev without destroying the peace she experienced at last. He was unsure of the solution, but he believed one would present itself. He was walking in dangerous territory, especially if he was wrong. In either case, he might be engaged in a losing proposition. Neev's disposition was difficult to discern. This meddling of his could ruin their friendship. Yet, he was driven to follow it to its conclusion, positive or negative.

His connection to the man who discovered the first bloom was also fascinating. The Coffee Table book was a testament to the ghost orchid's impact on this man as well. Roger received a second picture of him standing with his published book, the ghost orchid on the cover; and his face remained firmly in Roger's mind. He enlarged the photograph to see it more clearly and further confirm his suspicions. Even though the beard concealed plenty, the resemblance was too close to be a coincidence; the face was all too familiar.

Roger sent two emails the day he read the article about the third ghost orchid, one to Neev and one to the amateur photographer.

"Neev, I hope your visit with Truse met all your expectations and that you are ready to travel again. I have some information that I would rather share with you in person. Please don't be upset with me, but I have some new and interesting information about your mother that I think will help you. At the same time, the ghost orchid bloomed once more, and I'm going to set up cameras again. I wondered if my favorite partner is willing to make one more trip to Florida to humor an old man. I'll make reservations at our favorite hotel and pick you up at the airport." He purposefully assumed she would agree.

The second email was sent to California.

"This may seem very strange to you, but I feel there is something mysterious about our ghost orchid that requires additional exploring. A third blooming is beyond comprehension; yet here it is, and I fear this may be the last. I appreciate the picture of you with your Coffee Table book, and I wondered if you might be traveling this way again. The orchid may continue blooming for another two weeks or so if the weather holds. The swamp has more to offer as the wading birds are returning along with other wildlife for the winter. You might have a chance to take more photographs than before. What do you think? Is a trip to Florida a possibility? You'll have to make a quick decision, but I think you will be surprised by more than just the photography."

Roger didn't receive an instant response from either of the email recipients, and he held off from calling. This was a request that had to be in words. His own anxiety for his meddling was making him poor company in his brother's house. He gathered up his equipment and went to the sanctuary to follow his own suggestion. There, in the main foyer of the building were two sets of matted photographs on display from the two previous sightings of the orchid. They both held unique memories for Roger. The first sighting came through the eyes of his new friend, the amateur photographer. The second sighting he shared with his beautiful Neev and learned with her the secrets that had haunted her life. He was yet to discover what the third sighting might hold.

Twenty-Four
A Mystery

Roger wasn't the only one who sent emails. Neev finally decided to use the address on the card she had treasured since first reading her mother's letter. She sent a simple email, "I think you and I have something in common. I'm not certain. Please send a return email if you like a mystery."

Once she hit the send button, it was too late to change her mind and retrieve the short note. She was committed now, and there was no stopping until the ride came to an end.

Roger's email caught Jack off guard. He believed his ghost orchid was just that, his. He reconciled himself to his love lost and savored his serenity by rushing his book. Self-publishing had its challenges, but speed wasn't one of them. Once he set the book in motion, he had the pictures selected and the book was done in just two weeks. His dedication to her was the orchid photo on the cover. It really did contain some of his best work. Now, he was faced with this strange turn of events.

He was honored that a famous photographer would encourage him to participate in a shoot. He didn't miss the fact that he had an opportunity here that was almost as rare as his beautiful flower. A rush of memory washed over him as though she was haunting him again. He hungered for a glimpse at some of the precious words they had shared, the unchained look at each other's lives as they talked through email. Long ago, he stopped going to their Internet email site, knowing it was a walk through pain and tears. He no longer took that walk since he felt her forgiveness.

However, he couldn't bring himself to close the account, either.

Just one more time, he said to himself as he opened the screen, and *once more before I die* seemed to echo back from the recesses of his mind.

"I think you and I have something in common. I'm not certain. Please send a return email if you like a mystery," appeared on the screen.

He clutched at his heart to still its beating. No one else had this email address except for her friend who sent the newspaper clippings long ago. This email site was the secret rendezvous shared only with his love. It felt like she reached out to him once more, one last time. It was so shocking he clicked the "x" button to take the email off the screen.

He opened the site once more: "I think you and I have something in common. I'm not certain. Please send a return email if you like a mystery."

It was still there, blinking at him, waiting for a response.

His shaking fingers, never very speedy on the keyboard, typed, "This is a private email address. Where did you get it?"

Of course, his hope for an immediate response was not to be realized. Nothing was returned. The shock kept him from reading anything saved from his love. His health was delicate lately, and he was finding this whole mystery business stressful.

"This is a private email address. Where did you get it?"

This was not the response Neev sought, but it was a response. She needed to think carefully about her answer. An immediate reply was not required. One thing she knew already: the address was valid. She may have just heard from her own father. Wisdom dictated careful consideration of the many possibilities before going any further.

Instead, she placed a call to Roger.

"Hello, Neev! You've caught me at a bad time. I'm actually photographing our ghost orchid. They frown on cell phones in this place. I've so much to tell you. Is there any way you can come here, just once more? I'll make it easy. I'll send you the ticket and all arrangements here will be handled by me. You just need to get on the plane. Will you do that for me?"

She had only one answer. "Yes. Send me the ticket, Roger. I'll be there one last time."

Before she left for the airport, leaving Truse behind in tears, she sent one more email. "I have an orchid to visit, so the mystery will have to wait. My mother gave me this email address. It may have been in error."

Jack checked every day for his mystery correspondent at his haunting email site, the one he hadn't the heart to close out. Though he had destroyed the phone, he couldn't delete their words. And here it was: the orchid again. Surely, it couldn't be the same ghost orchid. Or could it? He sat at the table and looked at the ghost orchid on the cover of his book for a long time. He felt it calling to him, just as it spoke to him in Florida. Roger's invitation was the catalyst he could not ignore.

How could he explain his sudden departure for Florida again? He didn't. He simply bought the ticket and left. At his age, he had the right to a spontaneous trip for photographs. He earned the right. This was his retirement. Everyone admired the book of photos he put together. It was amazing how professional they looked after publication. It was worth the cost, every last cent. What was money for now but the simple pleasures? That was one more thing she said; she enjoyed the simple pleasures. Her words had become part of his very essence.

He knew one hotel, The Palmetto. While the memories would haunt him, perhaps they would comfort him also. His rental car was waiting at the airport for the short drive to the hotel. It suddenly dawned on him that he really hadn't set an appointment with Roger. Somehow it didn't seem to matter. He would send him a quick email from the hotel. If they could meet that was great. He had reservations for a week. That should give him time for a few more photographs. It was too bad he missed the second blooming, but at least he would have two unique experiences, two bloomings of a very rare phenomenon. He was both apprehensive and excited about visiting her swamp again. Theirs was a love that transcended time and space, life and death. It could not be denied.

The next morning was cool for Florida, in the mid 60's. However, the weatherman said to expect temperatures in the high 80's. He was dressed for the occasion with a couple cold bottles of water and sufficient gear to take great pictures. He even carried a new lens. This was the excitement of new adventure reminiscent of a more youthful time in his life. This was living. His excitement built as he neared the entrance. He was alive with expectation.

Roger met Neev at the airport, on time, his heart skipping a beat as she stepped through the doors. He was prepared for her usual complaints about the taxi or the flight or some other inconvenience along the way that cost her time and patience. Instead, she greeted him with that electric smile he loved and nothing but good news about her seat on the plane and the smooth connections. The usual two rooms were reserved at The Palmetto.

By the time they reached the hotel, a light dinner and a good night's rest were their choice. Roger still reeled from Neev's particular good humor. She must have found some type of resolution to her anger at last.

The next morning they drove to the swamp early to catch the only two blooms at sunrise, a picture they didn't have yet. Neev waited for Roger to tell her all the information he seemed busting to share by email and phone. Instead, he was very quiet, indeed. Everything was centered on the ghost orchid. That was okay with her. She still needed to tell him about sending the emails.

Three people stepped out of two cars just before sunrise, walked up the path toward the boardwalk and stood at two opposite sides of the counter at the same time. The female guide collected their twelve dollars each and told them the scope was set up, so they could easily find the orchid. Neev looked across the counter at the chiseled features on the face of the older man with a full, neatly trimmed beard who was looking intently at her. As usual, she smiled that all-encompassing smile that took in the world and made it hers. He couldn't help but smile. Roger saw, even if they didn't. He knew. He felt it deep in his soul. If this man wasn't her father, he was a dead ringer. He was a brother, an uncle, some relative. The resemblance was too uncanny to miss. They were apparently oblivious to the situation or Roger's thoughts.

"Isn't this a coincidence!" he and Roger said in one breath, laughing at their own joke.

The two bearded men shook hands like long lost friends and Roger introduced Neev as they walked toward the boardwalk.

Together, they continued down the path to the scope. Roger held back a little so they walked just ahead of him. Two slender frames with pride in their steps, his from years of military service, hers from modeling, walked nearly side by side for a precious moment in time, marked by a cool breeze just before they reached the ghost orchid.

High in the crotch of the same ancient bald cypress, where one bold branch reached out from the trunk, the two blooms were only visible through the scope and quickly erected camera lens. One a little higher than the second, the tendrils floated across the gossamer flower, the rising sun shining through the delicate petals. There they were, dancing in the morning breeze, stepping out from the tree's trunk and the root base that was barely visible. All three photographers enjoyed the personality exhibited high in that tree, the top flower leading its partner in the sensuous dance of life. Hypnotized by the scene, the audience of three smiled, feeling the life force pulsing through the swamp and exhibited in this orchid that had persevered through three separate blooming cycles when every other ghost orchid in the universe was lucky to have one bloom in one year, if at all. The miracle that brought these three people to this spot on this day was like all miracles, beyond explanation.

The whispered conversation turned to photography: the angle, the light, the zoom, the time exposure and other more technical terms. Each photographer helped the other, with no respect for experience or unique expertise. The challenge was finding the perfect subject in the perfect light. Each believed they had found both.

The sun's ascent into the cloudless sky heated the swamp and stirred up the natural breeze from the contrasting temperatures and pools of cool water from the rain. The alligators called to each other, louder as the sun rose higher in the sky. The wading birds stepped through the pools and darted after tiny minnows. Anhingas already perched in the branches where they dried their wings in the breeze before diving again. Turtles peeked through the swamp lettuce and climbed up on the logs. Bright red hibiscus added contrasting color to the verdant green; purple water hyacinths competed with the swamp lettuce for the water below. In all this waking life, the fuzzy cypress leaves, tinged with brown, dropped to the boardwalk where they crunched underfoot, as the canopy shed its cover, leaving the tall trunks barren for winter. The massive ferns were also turning brown. Suddenly, from nowhere, a little scud cloud dropped a quick morning shower as the photographers raced to protect their equipment, laughing at their predicament. The sun never stopped shining, a rainbow spreading its arch across the marsh in the distance. This was, at last, the moment they all awaited, the perfect light and the perfect subject.

Twenty-Five
Redemption

Roger suddenly clutched at his chest, and with a slight moan, fell to the boardwalk. Neev instantly hovered over him, attempting to resuscitate him as their new friend called on the cell phone for help. The quiet swamp became a bedlam of activity as the EMTs rushed down the boardwalk and picked up where Neev left off, running the gurney back down the walkway to the waiting helicopter. The nearest hospital was over fifty miles distant. The EMT told Neev to drive; there was no room for her. She handed the EMT Roger's wallet and started for the Kia Sportage, the amateur photographer not far behind.

"Let me drive you," he called after her. "We can return for your car later. Where are you staying? I'm at a hotel named Palmetto, not too far from here near the Gulf."

"Drive!" was all Neev could say as they tumbled into his rented Toyota, Neev pushing hastily gathered camera gear, with the contents falling, into the back seat.

"Turn right at the highway and don't stop until you reach the hospital."

As soon as Neev was certain they were headed in the right direction, she continued their earlier conversation. "We're at The Palmetto also. It's pretty much the only hotel of some elegance within reasonable distance from the swamp. What a terrible ending to a perfectly wonderful morning. For the first time in years I felt as though life was giving me the gift of serenity, and now this. It just proves that nothing is certain except death. Can you drive faster? I think they said he was being taken to North Collier. Please hurry. I know Roger has family near here. Once we get to the hospital, I should try to reach them."

He drove as fast as the two-lane, narrow road would allow. The terror in her eyes, reflected in the rear-view mirror, was almost more than he could bear. Whatever the relationship between Neev and Roger, her concern was grave. He would figure out the relationship later.

The hospital was not very cooperative. Neev was not a relative and not given access to any pertinent information. She went to great lengths to at last reach his brother on the island. They would rush to the hospital immediately.

He sounds really nice, thought Neev, with relief. It was strange that she knew none of Roger's family in all the years they had traveled together. Like her, he didn't indicate that he had strong family ties. She didn't know where his son and daughter lived but hoped the brother would handle any communication to them. She was under the impression that his son was in the military service.

She told her new friend that he could leave her. She would take a taxi to the hotel. He wouldn't hear of it. They sat together in the lobby and waited in silence. After what seemed like an eternity, a man and woman entered the lobby. Neev noted the man's strong resemblance to Roger. She listened as he spoke to the registration desk; yes, it was Roger's brother.

Neev stepped up to the couple. "Hello! I'm Roger's partner, Neev. We were photographing ghost orchids in the swamp when he passed out on the boardwalk. These people won't tell me anything! Can you?"

"I'm Craig; and this is my wife, Tanya. They said he had a stroke; the next few hours are critical. Did he tell you he's had small strokes in the past?"

Neev was angry. No, he had not told her anything. She'd had to figure out the arthritis herself. "No, he didn't tell me. I only knew he was taking fewer assignments and talking about retirement. I'm so grateful you're here!"

"We tried to reach his son and daughter. His son is in the military, traveling in Russia at the moment. We've notified them both. Hopefully they will get back to us soon."

The brother and his wife left for Roger's room and returned shortly. "The doctor says he will be in intensive care until morning. It's policy to keep him there twenty-four hours. He is breathing normally; all his vital signs are strong. We'll stay through the night if you need to go to your hotel or anywhere. Give me your cell number and I'll let you know if anything changes."

Neev reluctantly agreed. She felt pulled in all directions and had pretty much ignored her chauffeur. She really needed to return to the swamp for the rental car, preferably while it was still daylight and while she had someone to drive her. She felt the stress from the ordeal, but the adrenaline would kick in soon.

"I'll sit in the back and see if I can make some headway with the camera gear we threw in so haphazardly," she said as she led the way out of the hospital.

Bags, backpacks, tripods and other gear were all in a jumbled pile. They were quite certain, however, that they had grabbed everything that belonged to all three of them. Sorting it out might be challenging. Fortunately, Neev knew Roger's gear almost as well as her own.

She sorted the small pieces from the larger ones and put them back in their cases. Everything seemed okay with no evident casualties. Those items she didn't recognize were set aside for her very quiet chauffeur who watched her in the rear view mirror.

This is good, he thought. *It will help keep her mind off her friend in the hospital.* He was amazed at how quickly he wanted to protect her.

One aging piece of paper stuck out of his camera bag, and Neev pulled it out to refold it and put it back. Her gasp reached the front seat.

"Local school board employee involved in fatal crash" was the opening line. There, in a beautiful photograph was her mother's face. Below, another picture showed the twisted metal remains of the car, upside down in the ditch. Before she read any further, she cried out, "Why do you have this story about my mother? Where did you get it? And why is it in your camera bag?"

The newspaper article had remained there since he first downloaded it from email just about a year ago. He had almost forgotten the secret hidden in the case. The desperation in Neev's voice frightened him. He pulled into the parking lot at the sanctuary, stopped and turned in the seat to face her.

"I never knew she had a child. I was with her not long before her death, and she never mentioned a child. Neev? That's an Irish name, isn't it?"

Tears gathered in the corner of his eyes as the immensity of the moment took hold. Yes, Neev was about the right age.

"Neev, did you recently send an email that said you were visiting an orchid?" he managed in a hoarse whisper.

Seeing tears in a grown man's eyes was enough to shake Neev's courage to continue, but she knew she had to know now or never. "Yes, I sent two emails. One was answered that my inquiry..."

"...was to a private email address," he answered for her.

"In my response to that one I said I was going to visit an orchid, that perhaps my mother had given the address to me..."

"...in error," he finished her sentence again.

He opened his door and then hers and pulled her from the back seat into a bear hug. Of course, how was he so blind? This was their daughter! He had so many unanswered questions; but for now, he had the child of the woman he loved for a lifetime in his arms; and he wasn't going to let go soon. Their child. He knew the meaning of her name. It was all so clear, now. Neev was the Irish word for heaven. That was how they described their days and nights together, *a glimpse of heaven*. Here was the proof.

Finally, he released his hold so she could breathe. Their eyes were glassy with tears. Neither knew what to say. The practical seemed appropriate.

"Perhaps we should see if any of our equipment was left

behind," Neev suggested; and they made their way to the main building to fill the space, the chasm left by years unknown to them.

They entered the building and the elderly man with the mustache and the white hair sat at his desk behind the counter. Once again, in the face of that beautiful young woman with the wild red hair, he saw his friend who loved the swamp. He had to say something this time.

"You know, young lady, you bear a strong resemblance to a woman who used to visit this swamp every day. We didn't know each other very well, but over several years of saying hello every day, you get to know someone a little. She was a writer, you know. I read some of her stories. I didn't want to say anything the last time you were here because it's sad that she's gone. There was a terrible accident at the sanctuary exit, and she died right there. For a long time afterward, a part of me kept expecting her to come through that door. Now, wait a minute, I didn't mean to start a flood here. You just reminded me of her, and I was startled into mentioning it. I'm sorry. I miss her."

The tears streamed uncontrolled down Neev's face. Her father put his arm around her shoulder and drew her closer.

"Well, sir, you are correct. That was my mother. If you don't mind, we're just going to take another look down the path to see that we have all our equipment. We left in a hurry this morning." She had a catch in her voice in spite of her resolve to move forward.

"Oh, no! Were you in the party that had to leave by helicopter? I guess I just said the wrong thing at the wrong time. I'm sorry! How is the old gentleman?"

"He'll be just fine. I should hear from them soon. Thanks for asking." As if in answer to the question, Neev's cell phone rang and the brother gave a good report on Roger's condition. How long he would remain in the hospital was unknown, but a positive recovery was expected.

With that said, Neev and her father started down the path

to the ghost orchid location. It really was not the equipment they sought, but rather the final resolution to their mystery. They glanced at each other as the cool air touched them just before they saw the scope.

"You look first," he said.

The two orchids were there still, beautiful and serene, just as they were in the morning. They looked different, somehow; more settled. They seemed to be closer together.

He remembered the bench where he and his love shared cell phone conversations and led Neev there. They sat for a moment in silence until an early barrel owl called to its mate, "Whooooo?"

This was Neev's favorite time of the day when the sun relinquished its responsibility to the night, the short twilight that she and Roger enjoyed so much in Venezuela. The swamp became quiet also except for an occasional tree frog or the low barking sound of the alligator. Just as the sun gave its last gasp, he looked at Neev. His eye caught the glint of her necklace, barely showing through the conservative V at the neck of her blouse. He wouldn't have noticed normally, but the unusual pendant was familiar.

"May I see your necklace?"

"Of course. It's a Celtic Cross. I don't usually wear jewelry; it's such a bother. However, this belonged to my mother. She was wearing it when I was born, so I believe it must have been meaningful to her. I've only had it since she died. It was put away for safekeeping and nearly forgotten. I received it on my last trip home, just before we came to photograph the ghost orchid. It's beautiful." She removed it and handed it to her father.

This was the necklace Truse removed from her friend's neck just before Neev's birth. With the trauma of illness and a newborn child, the necklace was forgotten. It wasn't until Truse received the box for Neev that she remembered the necklace. She held it back for awhile, though, waiting for the right time. Perhaps she would be redeemed for loving Neev too much by returning the Celtic Cross to the Irish child…

"I'm glad you're wearing the necklace. I gave it to your mother as an expression of my love, a celebration of the Irish heritage we had in common." He touched the pendant to his cheek and returned it to Neev, tears filling his eyes once more.

From her purse she pulled the worn picture of a young man in a beard on a snow-covered ski slope. She looked at the picture and at her father. Yes, they were one and the same. She handed him the picture, smiling now through the tears.

"Well, I think it's time for some new photographs." He smiled. "What do you think, Neev? Roger might want to share in that session; he has brought us together as surely as the ghost orchid called to each of us."

Yes, new pictures were a good idea. Maybe someday, she might even share her mother's letter. Today, she just savored the end of the quest; the perfect moment that Roger knew would change their lives. He was right again.

"Yes," she said as they both looked up through the canopy at the rose tinged clouds from the setting sun.

Her mother's spirit transcended time and space, even death itself. Perhaps death is certain, but love is eternal.

Twenty-Six
Death

Neev wondered if death would ever leave her door. First, Rolf left her; then everyone else she loved: her mother, Truse and now Roger. He rallied some after the scare in the swamp, and officially retired to Florida where his brother and sister-in-law made him a welcome guest in their home. Neev's contacts with her father were sporadic, unlike the dreamlike vision she carried so long in her heart of the two of them sharing holidays and dinners.

He could not completely resolve in his mind how to bring her into his very structured life without causing trouble among his existing family and friends. He was a bit self-righteous in his pursuit of happiness in a responsible manner, taking care of everyone and causing as little distress as possible to anyone along the way. While his friends and relatives all had secrets that fell into the open, he was a master at revealing nothing but the best of his character. He was a model to his family of responsible citizenship and caring family relations. Neev was a threat to his self-image and to all else he held dear. His distress at his inability to resolve his situation was emotional and physical. He wasn't fair to Neev. Trying to find resolution nearly broke him for a while.

To help free her father from his obvious discomfiture, Neev accepted an impossible array of freelance photographic assignments to exotic global locations far beyond the reach of her father's dilemma. They parted with little discussion of the woman they shared, both too fragile from the loss, from the years of her life denied to them both, unknown to either except from Neev's few pieces of paper and his brief emails. She shared her photography and the travels with him through the secret email account he had shared with her mother.

For him, the email correspondence was a combination of joy and sorrow. He still expected the email to carry the signature lost to him forever even though he took comfort in the gift of this exceptional daughter they shared.

Sometimes, if their schedules permitted, they met for dinner in Hawaii or Italy or another of the favorite haunts of each. Their meetings were, however, rare. One such time, he had a Miami layover and Neev had plans to meet Roger. She and her father zipped through the Everglades on an airboat, dogs from the Indian Reservations barking in harmony with the complaining alligators and the disturbed calls of birds in flight. They dined on stone crabs in Everglades City. In spite of her vow to always hate Florida, the mystical Everglades worked their way into her soul just as they had captured her mentor, Roger. Both her father and Roger were part of this Everglades mystique that started with her mother.

Her father planned to attend Roger's funeral in Florida. Neev was returning from a stint in the Middle East. Her emotions were mixed: pain for the loss of Roger and anticipation at the prospect of time with her father. They had so much in common and shared so little. Maybe this time he would open up to her about the years apart from her mother, the unanswered questions that her mother's brief notes did not explain. Funerals had a way of opening old wounds and bringing back memories, joyful as well as sad.

She had only returned to Florida the one time since Roger moved in with his brother. They kept up a lively email and text messaging correspondence though. She was not ready for his death. It seemed he would live forever. She still looked at her cell phone, expecting his "ta da" and a chirpy message to appear. She would always carry his love in her heart though she was never able to return it in full measure. She was resigned to a life alone.

Her photography filled her passionate side.

September was a time of weather confusion in Southwest Florida, from anticipated hurricanes to drenching rain and humidity broken with dry days and an occasional cool evening off the edge of a thunderstorm. The sky was alive with great splashes of bolt lightning and loud cracks of thunder. Florida was known for its lightning strikes. Some nights, the air was alive with thunder and lightning without a drop of rain, humidity thick as clouds. Heat lightning filled the southern sky, sometimes lighting fires in the Everglades unknown to any but the animals that resided there. Other times, the sky filled with thick smoke as if the entire State of Florida was on fire. Thunder rolled through the Everglades and released torrents of rain that raised the water levels almost even with the boardwalks. Fear of fire was erased momentarily.

Jack arrived in Florida a day before the funeral, a room reserved at The Palmetto. The SUV ride from the airport was dreadfully lonely. He was repeating the ride from the airport to The Palmetto, the ride to the Everglades, the search for the orchid, year after year. He had been lucky the previous year when he and Neev met in Miami. They traveled together to the ghost orchid's second blooming that season. Sturdy yet delicate, white ghosts danced their choreography to the cacophony of tree frogs and woodpeckers, an occasional "Whooo?" echoing through the cypress canopy. By the miracle known only to the three of them, the ghost orchid continued to bloom year after year, July, August and September.

It was fitting that September was the month for Roger to experience his final stroke and leave this earth during the ghost orchid's last gasp. Their common interest in the ghost orchid and the beautiful Neev they shared was the basis for their unusual friendship from opposite shores across 3000 miles, one a photographer of redwoods, mountains and cascading streams, the other devoted to the rainbow colors of buntings and unique flowers known only to the Everglades. Roger's death was shocking even though Jack was well aware that Roger's recovery from the stroke in the Everglades was never complete. How would he comfort Neev? She had so many losses in her young life, and who would help her shoulder this new grief? He had an answer; he hoped she would find it as phenomenal as he did.

He arrived in Florida a day before the scheduled funeral. There was purpose in his schedule: he wanted to visit the Everglades once more before saying "good bye" to Roger. He was relieved as he started his walk on the boardwalk; the cool Everglades were welcome compared to the heat and humidity of the September afternoon. He had a cart this time to haul his camera equipment. This might very well be his last trip. His skill with photography had grown exponentially with the internet tutoring of his new friend. He learned to use the software that enabled time exposures to be overlaid, bringing all aspects of a scene into crystal clear focus. He hoped his orchid was blooming so he could apply his newfound skills. Along the way, he stopped to photograph a blood red swamp hibiscus and a large, white swamp lily. The rain's nourishment sent the ferns and alligator flags into the air like those found in a prehistoric jungle just waiting for the dinosaurs to break through. The water hyacinths painted the lettuce lakes with bright purple in sharp contrast to the thick, white swamp lilies on their sturdy stems fighting for light above the ferns and flags.

Twenty-Seven
Resurrection

Jack knew to expect the pressure of the humidity on his chest, the reason for the equipment cart. He set up his camera at the ghost orchid's best vantage point. The afternoon sun caught on the petals of two fragile blooms. The last bloom of the season was always smaller. He knew she was part of this spiritual journey, and he knew she spoke to him through the ghostly orchid. He came to accept this as clearly as he put his cell phone in his pocket each day and grabbed his cap. He wondered what message was carried in the two flowers. Then he saw one more deep green bud. September was always just two delicate, smaller flowers. Would this year be different? He stared at the third bud as though wishing it to bloom would make it so.

Neev expected to see her father at The Palmetto. He was not in his room. She thought about driving to the Everglades; she actually drove in that direction but at the turn to the sanctuary, she continued driving past as if somewhere else called to her. She continued to the highway that led south to Everglades City. No, she wasn't going to the sanctuary today; she would go instead to the lodge where she and Roger had dined when they followed the clues that led her to reuniting with her father. It was fitting that she go to one of his haunts, a place where he and his family often dined, not too far from their island home.

By the time she reached Everglades City, the sun had dropped toward the horizon and the air was thick with humidity. She felt the rain in the air as she climbed the old stairs to enter the cool, dark entry. Dazzling, varnished floors and walls lined with newspaper clippings were among the features that dated back to the 1800's when presidents and CEO's escaped to the Everglades from their urban drama. This was a place of simple luxury, previously catering to the wealthy and highly placed fishermen and hunters, a lodge in the exotic Everglades, far from the hustle and bustle of competitive corporate and political life in the northern climate.

Two long bars trimmed in padded black leather were off to each side. The center was dominated by the billiard tables and a gigantic fireplace, certainly not needed during this heat wave. She imagined a night in the winter though, billiard balls clicking, the fire roaring in the background. She continued through the lobby to the contrasting whitewashed screened porch, Bahamas fans were the only cooling force besides the growing gusts of wind from the ominous black clouds. She decided to order a light dinner, teriyaki strips on Caesar salad, as the sky opened up and rain came in torrents. The river raced past, carried by the tide and the pounding rain and braved by the fishermen on their shallow skiffs dressed in canary yellow rain gear.

"The tide is so fast a person attempting to swim across would likely drown," shared the young waitress who had quietly picked up the menu in front of her.

"Is it racing to or from the Gulf?"

"To the Gulf right now, and the rain is sending it even faster. Those fishermen are heading for the Gulf as well, dangerous for them also. May I get you something to drink?"

"No, just ice water, please. I'm ready to order. I'll have the teriyaki strips on Caesar. Please bring the dressing on the side." She was hungry that moment, but she didn't know how much she would actually be able to eat.

The rain poured down, thick and furious. She barely saw the fishermen in their skiffs just beyond the river's edge. Waiting for her light supper, Neev settled back for a long and thoughtful meditation in the storm. She had no desire to drive through the swamp on that dangerous two-lane road in this pounding rain. Instead, she framed the house across the river in her photographer's eye and wondered how to capture the ambiance of her restaurant with the lighting so poor. It was eerie with just the waitress for company on this huge, wrap-around southern porch, the clatter of rain mixing with the whirring fans.

Neev was the only diner. Surely someone was in the kitchen anyway. Of course, she was never alone. Even through the rain she hauled her photo gear into the club. When the rain stopped, she would take some photographs. The City Hall on the turnabout was a great shot. She had seen movies with this tiny crab fishing community as a backdrop. She drove by the crabbing boats on the way to the club. Crabbers were repairing nets and painting the bright red and yellow buoys in preparation for the October stone crab season. They waved at her as she passed.

Dinner was a long, savory meal. The rain continued like summer music as the river swelled, climbing higher, overrunning its banks and crawling up the shore toward that old southern home across the river. On her side of the river, the dock was nearly even with the water that rolled onto the sidewalk in waves as fishing boats continued in the rain toward the Gulf. She wondered if she should worry about the road home becoming too swamped to travel, but knew better. This rain was common here. The newer homes were up on stilts, the older on high foundations. The water would drain quickly from the road into the rivers and canals. What was uncommon was this much rain in September.

Time passed, as it should, with pleasant thoughts and ambiance. The waitress arrived unobtrusively to clear away the plates and leave the affordable bill. She refilled the welcome ice water, took away the billing folder with the exact change and tip. The rain finally stopped, just in time for the clouds to open a space so a piece of moon slipped through. Otherwise, the evening was black and dark and a little sinister.

Neev faced a long and lonely drive back to the hotel in the dark. It was better than rain, anyway. Florida twilight lasted no longer than sunset, none of the long, lingering twilight evenings of the north. Once again, she was reminded of the jungle evenings with Roger, their favorite time when night and day crossed paths. Within a few minutes daylight disappeared and the black night appeared. She whispered,

"Good night, Roger."

She moved her chair closer to the screen and watched fireflies wink their psychedelic green lights. She could not help but smile at their courtship, a voyeur, watching their romantic antics. The female remained on the vegetation while the male flew above, flashing his desire to mate with a female. If she liked the flashing light, she flashed back as a signal to mate, right then. If only finding a mate were that easy! These were the times when she still wondered if there was a mate out there somewhere, flashing his light toward her. Did she have enough light left in her soul to respond?

The time arrived for the drive back to The Palmetto. Hopefully her father had returned. They always enjoyed each other's company and at least shared the time since their last visit, comparing notes on their current photography subjects. Her father had actually entered a contest or two and published a second Coffee Table book. He might list this one for sale on eBay—might—with her encouragement. Their understanding of each other was growing. Before, Roger was always a central figure in their conversations. How could they talk about him now without her bursting into tears? She noticed that lately she was prone to crying anyway, to feeling life more deeply than she wished. Her desire for detachment seemed destined to soften her heart instead.

What a dark drive back to the hotel. The signs for panther crossings and the wide, water-filled ditches along the road gave rise to fears headlights might reveal either a panther or alligator sauntering across the road. The little sliver of moon had long since disappeared behind the lingering rain clouds that continued to mist the windows and hang fog-like in the headlights. The night felt like tears, tears for her Roger whose photography brought her a father and surrounded her with more love than she could have imagined. Roger would not want her sadness. His instructions for his death asked for no funeral, just a quiet memorial in a chapel near his beloved swamp and a joyful gathering of his friends and family.

With gratitude, she pulled into the hotel's underground parking. She wandered into the lobby bar and was pleased to see her father. He was still a striking figure of a man, slender and straight in bearing, thinning white hair neatly trimmed, and that mischievous smile escaping Jack's lips as he looked at his daughter, more like her mother with every passing year. He held a glass of wine, barely sipping it. He was lost until Neev entered the room. This hotel carried too many memories. Staying here was a mistake. Perhaps it was his own personal purgatory to feel the ache, the flood of memories that would always haunt him as sure as his orchid ghost. They were more haunting at The Palmetto. Neev was exquisitely beautiful, the same age as when he and her mother met. The emotions of this weekend were just about more than he could bear.

"Neev!" He stepped from the bar so they could embrace. He wondered when he should tell her. She no longer needed to live in the shadows. He told his family that he too had a deep and painful secret, released in the Everglades. He was not just the man they knew but he had a past buried deep within. He told them in the simplest terms about a past love and a daughter he had not known who came into his life through the most mysterious of circumstances.

It was difficult but he was surrounded by the same generous and loving family members that reflected his own generosity of spirit. They were shocked, and life was awkward and cool for quite a while as this unexpected turn of events took hold and a feeling of betrayal was overcome. In the end, as he prepared for his solitary journey to Florida, his family told him to bring her home. They would try their best. After all, this mysterious Neev was a half-sister, an aunt, a niece…certainly they could not leave her alone. The last hug he received before departure was laced with a whisper, "bring her home."

He did not know when to tell her. It seemed perhaps that after the funeral would be the best, a time when comfort would call for this new revelation. They moved from the bar to the lobby and made their plans for the trip to the Everglades the next day.

Neev also felt the ghosts of nights past at The Palmetto. Yet, when she crawled into the bed, exhausted, she was comforted by the plump down ticking surrounding her tired body; and she dreamed of the days when Roger's arms were the comfort, the days when their love was new, the fascination exciting and the future wide open. She had no regrets. His presence in her life was close to that of a guardian angel that brought her life full circle and didn't leave her until she found her history, a history that was still not totally revealed. He gave her a priceless gift and her heart would always beat a love song for him.

Morning broke with full sun in skies blue and cloudless. She met her father for breakfast though neither could do much damage to the buffet. She looked around the room, wondering if anyone else attending the intimate memorial would be staying at the hotel. Roger's children were staying with their aunt and uncle. Would his ex-wife attend? He had said she never remarried. In fact, in recent years, they seemed to find some common ground again and overcame the bitterness. Age seemed to do that. Neev had only met Roger's brother and his wife; the rest of his estranged family remained a distinct mystery.

The passion of youth, when everything matters so much, allows for hate to grow as rapidly as love and tarnish all that it touches. At some point in life's journey, only love matters, all the tarnish from past injustices disappears in favor of the shine only loving hearts can reveal. It was just such relief that filled Neev when she released the anger toward her mother. Life continued to reveal to her that all choices are not as simple as they appear. Love takes many different roads. Maybe now that she knew she had the love of her parents she would be able to love herself. That was the first step in loving another. She thought again about the fireflies, a smile turning at the corner of her mouth in spite of the heavy heart with which she faced the day.

"I'm glad to see you smile," her father said as she settled in beside him in the car, leaving the hotel parking lot for the small chapel in the Everglades. "You remind me more of your mother every time I see you. It's not that you look so much like her, but your smile fills your whole face just like hers. Know that I loved your mother with a heart so full that it was near breaking. Life with regrets is not my choice. I fight regrets about you and your mother. I hope someday to really tell you everything. I kept a few journals along the way, actually your mother's idea, nothing consistent for sure, but maybe I can share them with you sometime."

"Mother kept journals. She left some pages for me that nearly broke my heart except that sharing them with Roger added one more piece to the puzzle that he solved for all of us. I believe, though, that nothing in life is pure coincidence. Every choice takes us racing toward a different future than another. Somehow, our choices have brought us together. I accept that. Like you, I am trying to not have regrets. Otherwise, I will cry forever about the lost years spent in anger."

With those words, they lapsed into silence as the highway narrowed and wound through the Everglades. She was first to spot the little chapel tucked in the palmettos.

Yes, Roger would pick this chapel. A nearby pond was filled with blooming, purple hyacinths, and a field of morning glories spread toward the horizon. Neev almost expected an owl to call "Whoo?" and for her to answer, "Roger."

Twenty-Eight
Metamorphosis

Neev was surprised to see so few people. She had expected someone from National Geographic, but she recognized no one. About 25 people gathered in the little chapel. She only knew Roger's brother and his wife. Neev and her father were seated by an usher. A collage of photographs taken by Roger was exhibited at the front of the chapel. Both Neev and her father saw the ghost orchid at the same time, a shot of a single orchid that jumped from the photograph. An attractive couple about Neev's age came in together. He wore a full dress uniform. Neev's heart nearly stopped. It was as though Roger had walked into the room. The resemblance was too close not to be Roger's estranged son. Likely that was his wife accompanying him, or did she also bear a resemblance?

Beautiful music began—a flute and a violin—and Neev stopped her musings. The music was soothing, very like the sounds of the jungles and swamps. His brother gave the eulogy. Roger would have liked the words, simple and without embellishment. This was a good man who loved nature and gave himself to his profession. He left a wife—Neev noticed that his brother mentioned the "wife"—and two children and friends and family who would miss him but would always be blessed by his view of the world. His legacy would forever tell of beauty that his photographs preserved for future generations. He would want joy, not tears, for his passing.

Neev could not help it, tears streamed down her face. An

attractive older woman with coifed gray hair was also dabbing her cheeks. Was this his ex-wife? She was lovely. The son and the woman with him were also having difficulty keeping their composure, but did not shed tears. They filed out of the chapel to picnic tables set with luscious, tropical fruits and juices, flavored coffees and teas. The music was now joyful, with a quick beat that raised the spirits. Smiles were coming out on the faces. Roger would prefer smiles to sadness.

"This is Roger's partner, Neev. Neev, I'd like you to meet Roger's son, Ray and his sister, Sandra." Neev was caught off guard as Roger's brother introduced them. Ray looked deep into her eyes, and they shared their loss right then. She could say little beyond, "Hello. My deepest condolences."

Sandra was not really ready to exchange conversation and hurried away toward the table, leaving Ray and Neev standing together, awkwardly.

"I understand you shared assignments in some of the most remote places he left us to photograph…"

She heard a touch of bitterness, but ignored it. "Roger was my mentor. He taught me to see beyond the first frame to the perfect subject in the perfect light. I'm sorry he traveled so extensively. He often spoke of you. You were never far from his heart even if you were far in distance."

Neev had no idea what information Roger had shared with his family, but she was going to believe that their relationship was a private matter, shared in remote places beyond the reach of gossip or misunderstanding. Their experiences together would remain just that, theirs. Love was a word without translation, just as death was without consolation. He would always live for her with every camera she touched, every photograph she examined. His expert eye would guide her thoughts; his touch would sooth her loneliness. Death would not take him from her completely.

She smiled that radiant smile that even Ray could not ignore, smiling in return.

"How long will you be staying here?" he asked with such

interest he surprised himself.

"It's strange, but I didn't book a return flight to anywhere. I'll check in with National Geographic, but first I want to go to the sanctuary and look for some more treasures to photograph right here where Roger found such beauty."

"Maybe I could tag along? I never understood his obsession with photography. I resented it all my youth. But in recent years, I have found some appreciation for his photographs, even growing to treasure some."

"Ray, this is my father, who was also a friend of Roger's."

"Hello, Ray. It's too bad we have to meet in these circumstances. I am sorry for your loss. Roger was an artist with a camera and actually helped me with my amateur attempts. However, it is his sideline as a detective that will endear him to me the rest of my life. I will miss him."

"Ray suggested he tag along to the sanctuary tomorrow."

"Neev and I plan to start our trek in the swamp around nine. We'll have all our own camera gear. Are you a photographer, too?"

"No, not at all. In fact, this is pushing my leave. I need to be back in the air by tomorrow night, a red eye flight. I want to go with you, though. I'll meet you at the main desk at nine. It's a little late, but I want to understand my father's obsession just a little. Maybe it will help me understand him as well."

"Great! I think we'll say a word or two and be on our way back. I believe we've said all we can today. Roger would understand our eagerness to leave here and prepare for the sanctuary tomorrow. We have a ghost orchid to photograph."

"Yes, he was obsessed with that ghost orchid. You should see the time overlays from this year's blooming. I have to admit, they are exquisite. You know, his last stroke was while he was developing these himself, black and whites. Maybe I'll get a chance to show you. I think they are his best. One was on display here."

"Yes, I would love to see them all. Your time is so short. Maybe tomorrow afternoon?"

Neev's excitement had her speaking too rapidly; she was also nervous. They were already leaving for their cars, but Neev called over her shoulder, "We're at The Palmetto, on the coast."

She wasn't sure whether Ray even heard her. Something compelled her to leave him with a way to contact her. Somehow the loss of Roger was softened by the contact with this replica, this younger version, this very attractive son, even if only for a day. Something needed to sooth her aching loss. Where would she ever find such a friend again? Even in their many separations, she always knew he was there. Now, he was not. Loneliness stole into her heart, and she wept silent tears.

Now, she had a father, an equally illusive person, seldom in her life but bigger than life when there.

"Well, that was quite an experience." He broke the silence on their long drive to the hotel. "Roger's son seems like a nice young man. I'm looking forward to our adventure tomorrow. Perhaps we'll also have time to see his time release stills of the ghost orchid." With no answer from Neev, he let her continue in her silence for the rest of the drive.

The next day arrived with an unseasonal morning storm. The air was fresh and cool as Neev and her father started their trip to meet Ray and visit the ghost orchid for what they both knew was one last time. Neither spoke of it; yet, each felt a sense of finality in everything they did from the time of their arrival in Florida. This ride felt like the last drive through the swamp. The stay at the hotel was sweeter and the food more delicious because it felt like a last meal at a favored resort. With each mile, the finality was more firmly felt by both in their unspoken quest.

True to his word, Ray was waiting for them, in uniform. He was afraid he might be racing for his plane.

"My duffle is in the car; I'm not taking any chances." Ray's smile filled his face and took both Neev and her father from their somber mood. "I have a surprise. I have my dad's ghost orchid photographs also. No one else really wants them, and since you seem as fascinated as he was... Perhaps you, Neev, may treasure them more than any of us. They are a gift to you. Someday, when I get another leave, maybe I might decide to reclaim them. For now, though, you are the custodian of my father's obsession. Does that work for you?"

Neev caught herself brushing away the tears brought on by this generous act of understanding. She impulsively hugged him; he hugged her in return, perhaps a little longer than either expected.

"That's thirty-six dollars for three adults." The ranger was someone new, logical in light of all the strangeness of the morning. They put all the camera equipment in a borrowed cart and started down the walk. Dew still danced on the green floor of the swamp, an occasional drop from the canopy overhead as little dewdrops gathered together.

"Oh!" Neev leaped to the other side of the boardwalk as a brown bear, more terrified than her, raced pell-mell through the trees.

In spite of the quiet, Neev's father and Ray burst into laughter, both talking at the same time. "I think the bear was more frightened of you than the other way around, even though I've never seen you move so fast. Poor Ray, you almost knocked him into the swamp!"

They were just passing the space where the fence had an opening for animals to cross over. As the first guests of the morning, they must have disturbed the sleeping bear under the boardwalk. At least the experience added levity to their morning.

The rest of the walk in the direction of the ghost orchid was in silence until they felt the chilling air that announced the ghost orchid was near. They looked at each other at the same time, wondering if it was felt by all. It was not imagination; a definite drop in temperature with a slight breeze was a fact. The ghost orchid was not much further down the walk. They moved hesitantly, as if it was truly a ghost they sought.

The guides had already set up a scope. The men let Neev look first. There, for the first time in the third blooming, were three lovely blooms—and one more bud, ready to break open. Not only were two blooms always the last of the season, there were never any additional buds.

"Look, you won't believe it!" Neev whispered with some excitement as she moved away from the scope, signaling her father to take a look, forgetting about Ray who had never seen the ghost orchid beyond his father's pictures.

It was an amazing view. The rising sun sent shimmers of light across the dew on the delicate, gossamer petals dancing in a slight breeze. The blooms, all three, were small and perilously perched at the ends of long, slender stems stretching away from the roots, wrapped around the tree. It appeared as if they were ready to take off, break free. Finally, he released the scope to Ray.

At first Ray had difficulty with the focus. Neev stepped up and adjusted it for him until he could see the orchid well. Her touch as she brushed next to him was electric. Her every move struck him as sensuous and arousing.

Ray's quiet voice was barely audible. "It's as if his pictures have come to life." He, too, was struck by the infinite beauty of the three ghosts in the morning sun. He saw his father here, peering through his own lens at this very flower with unexplained fascination. In this moment, he felt closer to his father than in most of his adult life. It took Ray's stoic nature to quell the groundswell of tears, the loss of his father's companionship, the aches of his youth, from pouring fourth in front of these strangers and this beautiful young woman.

He stepped back.

"A bench is not far away." Neev saw the need for comfort and would do her best. "We could step over there while he sets up his camera. Then I'll set up mine. You'll get another chance to look then. Come on."

"Sure, go ahead. I'll have my camera set in a minute or two."

Neev took Ray's hand in hers and they walked the few feet to the bench overlooking the dry lakebed, populated with a world of ferns and fronds with a few bright red swamp hibiscus and delicate white cymbidium.

"Look, there's a swamp lily. That one is particularly beautiful, filling the stem with blooms. I think that's in honor of Roger." She smiled at Ray and he was filled with her. He shivered.

Neev felt him shiver by her side and moved closer. She thought perhaps the damp, cool breeze had reached him. Perhaps it was the memory of Roger. Perhaps it was the swamp's power. In any case, they sat in silence, holding hands, eyes avoiding each other, until they saw her father walking in their direction.

"It's the strangest thing. By the time I had the camera set up and looked through it, the fourth bloom broke through the bud. It's small and tenuous, but it's there. You must look. I've taken many pictures already. You might want to just use my equipment. It's too amazing to take the time to set up yours. You can change lenses on my unit."

Neev and Ray continued to hold hands as they approached the camera. High in the canopy overhead danced not two, not three, but four ghosts, one just bursting forth from its bud. Neev's father stepped back and felt the cool breeze swirling all around. Before him, Neev shared her photo knowledge with Ray, the two so engrossed in her photos and their subject that he was forgotten.

But Jack was not forgotten. Once more, he felt that all encompassing sense of wellbeing he felt the first day in the presence of the ghost orchid. She was here. She was sending him a message. At last she could rest in peace. All she had taken from Neev in her grief was returned. Redemption was at hand. Neev had her father. The laughter of the two young people struggling to get the perfect picture echoed through the swamp.

That afternoon, they pored over Roger's pictures at the Club until Neev and Ray raced across Alligator Alley so Ray could catch his plane in Miami. Neev's father drove alone back to The Palmetto where he planned to join her for breakfast in the morning. He wasn't alone. He had the pictures. He had his ghost. He saw his love in Neev. He would never be alone; neither would Neev.

Twenty-Nine
Family

At first Neev and Ray denied their attraction, basing their denial on the discomfort that was obvious. Eventually, nothing could keep them apart: not wars, or distance or fear. Their attraction was stronger than any objection. They were married just six months after Roger's death, a whirlwind romance with nuptials on the edge of the Grand Canyon and a honeymoon whitewater rafting on the Colorado with Neev attempting photography to save the memory. At last, she felt all the sweeping emotions of love that she thought were not in her destiny.

Ray was an attentive lover and generous man who convinced her immediately that they must have children. While he was stationed in Russia, Neev gave birth to Jay, a beautiful boy with alabaster skin, hair so blond it was almost white and eyes that became more piercingly blue with each passing month. Ray was near bursting with pride. The best part was his imminent retirement. He would be able to help Neev raise their son while he decided what venture would help them build a future for their little family.

"Yes, yes, you must come and see Jay," insisted Neev to her father. "Somehow, he is much like you. We'll only be in the States for a short time. Then, we're off to Italy for Ray's last duty."

She had not seen her father since Roger's death. The whirlwind romance with Ray, the marriage, the birth of Jay; life just seemed to fill up. The obsession with finding her father was now quelled. She knew he existed and she was loved. They never talked about his life in California. It seemed like he stepped through a mirror and disappeared into a world unknown to her. She didn't ask, and he didn't volunteer.

He never found the right time to tell Neev that she was no longer a secret. The entrance of Ray into her life eliminated the need for him to provide her with a new life to help her overcome grief. She found her own joy with Ray. She was so accustomed to her father's second life that she did not provide an opening, rushing off to her newfound romance. The birth of this grandson marked the end of his own secrets, logged faithfully in journals still hidden in the false back of the gun cabinet. He no longer felt compelled to chase the ghost orchid. With Neev's marriage, the ghost in the orchid's work was done. Neev was surrounded with her own family and love from every direction. Redemption was at hand all around. His surprise for Neev could wait a little longer.

"What do you mean you have a new grandson? After causing us so much pain and discomfort months ago, you never told her? You have waited until she has a husband and a son? And now you want to invite them here? Well, I must say; when you have a bomb to drop, the explosion isn't small.

"Okay, invite them here. We're ready. We'll make it work."

"Did you notice? Jay is a combination of your name and Ray's. We honored you both, and he carries Roger's middle name, Charles. Jay Charles Andrew. You won't believe it, but we call him JC for short already." Neev's joy radiated around her.

Father and daughter were sitting at Starbucks, drinking their favorite latte with Jay in his child seat, sleeping peacefully while Jack contemplated telling Neev at last that her world was growing bigger. His heart raced with anxiety. He hoped for the best. He picked them up at Neev's little bungalow on the base after she returned a few days ahead of Ray.

As if on cue, Jay opened his eyes and puckered up to cry. Neev lifted him to her breast and gave him the milk he craved. Her father watched in awe. This was his beautiful photographer daughter, the picture of domestic bliss. She looked so happy that he couldn't help but glow himself. He was still going to wait for the right moment.

The right moment did not arrive. He returned to California without telling his daughter once more, and his heart gave out. There was no warning, no evidence of pain. He was believed to be in excellent health. It was a massive heart attack and he could not be revived. This ordinary man died without telling his precious Neev that his secret was open, that she was welcome in his family.

Neev discovered her loss because there were no answers to her emails. Finally, she called the emergency number he had left with her for those times when Ray was out of the country. She had never dialed the number. The young woman who answered, his California daughter, told Neev that their father was gone. She offered to hold the funeral until Neev arrived. She tried to be kind to Neev, lost in her own grief and lack of understanding as to how her father had not told Neev about his family or that she was welcome to know them. The awkward conversation only added to the grief.

"Don't put a hold on the funeral," Neev said through sobs. "I would be uncomfortable among strangers. My family does not belong in California. My husband arrives today. Perhaps we can talk again later. I almost feel as if I have done something wrong, yet, I am as much his daughter as you. It may take us some time to adjust to this without his help. Thank you for your kindness."

Ray provided comfort to Neev. With his help, she started some communication with her California relatives. When Ray retired, they accepted an invitation to visit her father's family. They learned to love them as the awkwardness passed. Resemblances were everywhere, and little Jay was a center of attention. The similarities and differences worked themselves out and melded into a family quilt that wrapped itself around Neev's life and gave her the love and comfort she had craved all her young life.

Ray's work took them East to New York. The world of

technology kept them connected even as the years drifted by. Eventually, Jay was traveling unaccompanied between New York and California, enjoying the extended family attention and adventures. Neev continued her photography. Their mutual careers made one child sufficient—the joy of both their lives.

Occasionally, Neev checked out the web site for the ghost orchid and learned that it stopped blooming. For years, the roots still clung to the tree, giving forth no blooms. She finally let go and looked no more...

Neev awoke with a start. She felt anxious, but relaxed a little seeing her peacefully sleeping husband at her side. She stepped onto the floor quietly and padded to Jay's room. He was sleeping peacefully as well, almost a miniature of his dad. No, nothing was wrong in the house.

It was July; perhaps the air conditioner had awakened her. This July was particularly hot. She swallowed a teaspoonful of Benadryl and went back to her bed and to sleep. She awoke late to the shrill ring of her kitchen phone. Ray already left for the office, dropping Jay at school on his way. Neev was alone.

Thirty
Eternity

An attorney called Neev. Apparently, something unsettling happened in California. The potential sale of the family home required parting with some of their father's things. Two in particular came to the attorney's attention. Jack's framed picture of the ghost orchid was a hiding place for a codicil to his will, formal and witnessed, that the attorney had not mentioned at the reading of the will proper. The codicil had no monetary impact at the time of his death. It was better left unread. The attorney did not have the original anyway. He assumed it was destroyed and no copies remained. He was wrong.

Another unsettling event came with the discovery of a false back in the gun cabinet. Computer disks and journals filled the back, all neatly catalogued and addressed to "Neev only. At my death."

The attorney felt it was absolutely necessary for Neev to be present for the reading of the codicil and to determine whether she wanted to accept the journals or leave them for his family. Everyone was upset about both events after so many scars had healed over the years. These unexpected revelations opened new wounds.

"As soon as I talk to Ray, I'll make travel arrangements." Neev's hands shook as she put the phone in its cradle. She was drawn to the den where she kept the pictures she treasured of Roger's precious ghost orchid. Even before checking into plane reservations, she spread the pictures out on the floor, especially the time release ones.

"Well, mother of mine, he is yours. He has released every last memento tied to me. You have him for eternity; I had him such a short time." Neev felt some sense of comfort from her talks with her mother. It wasn't the first time she had pulled out those pictures for a conversation. Today, this process was her only comfort.

She called Ray. Much to her relief, he took over with the reservations. She was a bit numb. It was a long way to California for the wrong reason. She planned to finally close the email accounts that had been continued from the days her father shared them with her mother. She kept thinking she might read what emails were still in the archives but also believed it would be an invasion of her parents' lives. Thus, the accounts remained open.

She wished he had lived longer to enjoy Jay more. Jay would be heartbroken that he could not travel with his mother. Even as a baby, his connection to his grandfather was amazing. He would just pick Jay up from his child seat and Jay was content. Since his passing, Jay's summers with his extended California family made a major impact on his thinking. He could hardly wait for school to end this year but was stuck with a short summer program before leaving for California. He would have to wait until August.

"Neev, I am so sorry you have to travel there under these circumstances, to reopen the past." Ray wrapped Neev in a bear hug as she dissolved into tears at last. Time ran since she reunited with her father, lost Roger, married Ray, gave birth to their beautiful son and lost her father. Where did that time go? Was it time that stole those she loved? Or was it something else?

The trip to California was uneventful. Not knowing the circumstances completely, Jay was left home in great distress. The reading of the codicil was terrible for all, but Neev was grateful Jay's future was set regardless of the path the family traveled. The codicil provided stocks that had been set aside in her name. That was it. No glowing words or explanation, just the legal terminology that would release those stocks to Neev. She saw them as Jay's future. Otherwise, she wouldn't want them. His family sat quietly for the reading and accepted her entitlement to his gift.

The journals from the gun cabinet created a more difficult decision. Perhaps they would reveal parts of her father's life that would provide comfort to this family. They were already in pain because they were so clearly addressed to Neev. They could also reveal more than this family might want to know.

"Here's my suggestion. I will take the journals home with me and decide there. I promise not to destroy any of them and to share anything that will give you comfort or insight that might be revealed."

The family that extended her such warmth now regarded her with some distance. She hoped time would once again heal all. The parting was cordial but lacked the warmth originally extended to Neev.

She returned to New York, exhausted. It was only temporary until their permanent move to Florida. Ray's new venture in computer technology was taking them to the east coast of Florida. Neev was coming full circle, from declaring she would never visit the state to actually residing there. Life had a way of working out its own plan in spite of hers.

Life returned to normal. Jay accompanied Neev on a couple photo shoots. He had an eye for photography and the patience necessary to capture just the right shot. Neev was pleased. They tromped through the Fakahatchee Strand in search of more ghost orchids, with no luck, and returned with mosquito bites and some photographs of wood storks. One of Jay's proudest pictures was a flock of roseate spoonbills rising from the swamp with the sunset painting the sky ablaze in the background and framing the flight of white and pink. She purposefully kept Jay away from the sanctuary where so many strange events surrounded the discovery of the ghost orchid. While her questions were answered she was haunted by the string of death's that followed her. She was keeping Jay to herself. His day would come.

An airplane ticket arrived for Jay; his summer treks to California resumed. He remained the California connection; Neev still felt estranged after the uncomfortable post-death incidents. She made a promise about the journals, but it was one she couldn't keep if she did not open them. The photograph that held the codicil was also Neev's, and she put it away with her other treasures.

Ray's business was successful. Birthdays passed and their lives were almost ordinary. Yet, daily, Neev was sinking. A cloud followed her, sapping her joy. She made a great pretence that everything was the same, but the pretence itself became more difficult, draining her energy further. On one of her more difficult days, when it was all she could do to send Ray off to work and Jay to school, her need to climb back in bed and sleep was winning.

Just as she was ready to succumb to the insurmountable depression, she thought about the portfolio of pictures. They always gave her comfort, drew her closer to the strength she wanted from her mother, reminded her of Roger. She smiled as she remembered Ray telling her that he would return on a leave and collect the pictures back; he collected her instead. She still had the pictures.

She walked thoughtfully to the buffet and pulled out the artist's case full of ghost orchids and spread the magnificent photographs across the living room floor. Something worked at her mind. She felt drawn to the sanctuary in spite of her reluctance. It was already September. Any possibility of blooms had past. Anyway, the ghost orchid had not produced another bud since the day she met Ray. Neev and Ray must have absorbed the plant's energy through their passion for each other.

Neev logged into the mini computer, "ghost orchid, Corkscrew" expecting nothing. Instead, a headline shouted from the local section of the daily newspaper,

"Surprise, the famous Ghost Orchid has at last decided to bloom again. Our photographer just captured its beauty before it disappears, two hearty blooms so close together that they almost appeared as one. They were only visible for a couple of days, and then seemed to evaporate overnight. Everyone hopes the rest of the blooms will yet appear."

The date of the blooming matched her sleepless night before the attorney's telephone call. The paper also advertised hotel packages with tours to the viewing site. The ghost orchid was the little sanctuary's main attraction. Many new signs and boardwalk improvements could credit the increased number of visitors for their funding.

The pictures were truly exquisite, the petals so close together they did appear as one grand flower. Neev stared in wonder. She scanned the papers and the sites as far back as they were carried in the archives. No more sightings were recorded, just a notation at the web site that, "We're still hoping for another ghost orchid bloom, apparently in vain. Since the brief hello in July, no further buds have appeared. Maybe next year."

Neev understood. The ghost orchid did not need to bloom again. Its purpose was fulfilled. They were together at last. Neev's hunger for roots was fully satisfied, and the guilt that separated her parents was released. Eternity was theirs to make up for their losses. Maybe someday she would take Jay to the swamp and tell him the story. She was only sorry she never really had the time to know more about her father to share with her son. A resemblance was growing as Jay left childhood for puberty. He was tall, slender and athletic with eyes that pierced the soul and a smile that won hearts.

The ghost orchid, however, remained in her heart to carry her through life's challenges, regardless of their complexity. She left the pictures on the carpet to share with her husband and son when they arrived home. Maybe, just maybe, she could share a little of her joy and sorrow. Her family was all here, in this house and in this room. Their strength would return her joy; she needed to ask them. Maybe they would encourage her to read the journals left by her father. She felt better with a plan. Was it her imagination, or did she feel a cool breeze through her hair as she organized the pictures, followed by that feeling of comfort and wellbeing she often sought but was denied?

The ghost orchid never bloomed again, but the plaque describing it remained at the site. Rumor had it that a cool breeze was sometimes felt just at the turn before the ghost orchid's location. People who experienced the breeze said they were overwhelmed by a sense of wellbeing. Guides who walked the boardwalk in the summer evening's humidity were certain they noticed the orchid's night aroma. Others said it was just the overall magic of the swamp. The roots, however, were still firmly wrapped around the trunk, high in the cypress canopy, waiting for another special day.

Many photographs, note cards and mementos in the gift shop celebrated their ghost orchid. Even one of Roger's photographs of the last two blooms of summer, taken one September, hung in the shop. The two blooms seemed to improve with age, watching those who wandered past the gift shop and into the swamp, seeking their own answers to life's unsolved mysteries.

Neev still had her single orchid photo, her father's photograph, but she was afraid to hang it anywhere. She was haunted by the words Roger overheard, spoken about the ghost orchid when it was first discovered. "The ghost orchid is often associated with death and the manifestations of the soul." The ghost orchid's mystery surrounded all those she loved and had lost. Her father's singular ghost orchid photograph was tucked away. She thought it was forgotten.

Jay asked for the picture after Neev and Ray tried to share with him the short version of their romance and the magic of the ghost orchid, deep in the Everglades. "Mom, may I have the ghost orchid picture from Grampa, the one from California? You didn't hang it anywhere. I'd like it for my room."

It was difficult for them to convey the complexity of the lives that changed the day the ghost orchid bloomed. Jay had many unanswered questions but decided to conduct his own search. He watched the newspaper and the sanctuary web site eagerly in late summer, in hopes the orchid bloomed. The camera his parents gave him on his birthday became a good friend. He was ready.

Late one evening, Jay noticed a light burning in the den. He peered through the cracked door and saw his mother curled up in front of the fireplace with a closed book in her hands and Grampa's ghost orchid leaning against the chair. His grandfather's journals that had been stored in the locked china cabinet were spread out on the floor all around her. Though he saw tears glistening on her cheeks, he slipped back to his room.

Unaware of the love in her son's heart as he left her with her thoughts, she opened the journal in her lap. A letter fell out, obviously old and yellowed. The envelope was sealed, but the glue had long ago dried and the flap opened easily.

"My Darling Mel," she read, "my passion for you is overwhelming. I must have you and need you in my life. You cannot leave and live a life of doubt forever pondering whether you have met your soul mate. While I know nothing is fair, I also realize that passionate, deep, physical and emotional love is seldom experienced in a single lifetime. Allowing you to escape from me is more than I can bear. I have searched in vain for you; I will not give up. I know you believed I was never coming back, but you are wrong. Once you entered my heart, I was captive. I will never let you go again. We are two hearts intertwined that will never separate from each...."

Neev's tears flowed. The letter fell to the floor as she tried to brush them away with the back of her hand. She felt like a voyeur, looking into the thoughts of her parents, the very love that gave her life. Here was the answer she had sought since childhood. Here was the love to fill the chasm in her soul. She looked at the journals spread around the chair. Her father was here. As she leaned over to pick up the letter and continue reading, a tear dropped onto the petals of her father's ghost orchid.

Epilogue

The rare ghost orchid of National Audubon Corkscrew Swamp Sanctuary was first discovered by a hiker looking for owls in early July 2007. The subsequent sightings brought this floral discovery to near Biblical proportions. The list of firsts continued their climb. This beautiful healthy plant with tentacle-like roots embraced the trunk of a huge, ancient, bald cypress tree 150 feet off the boardwalk and about 45 feet into the canopy above. The paper-thin petals appeared like gossamer dancers or ghosts, reaching out from the crotch of the tree branch, dancing in the swamp breeze. They appeared detached from the tree, floating in space. No green leaves were visible.

The discovery in July was a rare occurrence. The ghost orchid, a native of Cuba and Southwest Florida, had never been seen in Corkscrew Swamp. The flower was the subject of quests in the Fakahatchee Swamp where it was known to have as many as ten blooms, but never more than one at a time. The Corkscrew Swamp ghost orchid, dubbed "Super Ghost" by many, carried eight to ten blooms from its first discovery; and they slowly died, leaving only a root system, tightly wrapped around the crotch of the tree, its green and brown color blending with its host.

In mid-August, the surprising ghost orchid bloomed again, this time with ten flowers showing at the same time, hardier and larger than the earlier discovery. They grew even further from the tree trunk, as if suspended in space. Large, healthy petals marked this truly surreal appearance. Still, the ghost orchid was not finished when the last of these blooms dried and fell away.

In mid-September as the winter wading birds returned to the swamp and the cypress began shedding the summer finery for a starker winter look, the ghost orchid bloomed once more. This time, only two, small weak blooms were visible. The mystical quality of this highly unusual third blooming was not lost on the visitors whose lives were touched by its magic and its mystery, some returning often to watch its development and demise. They gathered in little groups to compare notes on first sightings, number of blooms and the best angle for photographs. Amateur photographers and professionals treated each other with the respect demanded by this endangered and rare species.

Ghost orchids were the subject of a book "The Orchid Thief" and subsequent movie, "Adaptation" yet, that author who searched for the ghost orchid during the writing of her book never actually saw the flower blooming in the swamp.

D. K. Christi spent three months watching the progress of the "Super Ghost" through all its mystery at National Audubon Corkscrew Swamp Sanctuary, from its first sighting in summer through the autumn of 2007. She was changed forever by the experience.

Those who follow this rare flower believe the root system may be over fifty years old. Why did it bloom in this decade? Why did it bloom three times, spreading its wonder from July through September, as it overlooked purple morning glories in the marsh below to fields of yellow, miniature sunflowers painting the marsh gold?

A year passed while *Ghost Orchid* filled the pages of the manuscript. This beautiful apparition of a flower bloomed on schedule in July, August and September of 2008. D. K. Christi's obsession was recorded and photographed by the *Naples Daily News* in an article about her search in the canopy for her "Orchid Ghost." On schedule, the ghost orchid bloomed again in July of 2009.

Maybe this story of love, hate and redemption is only one possibility for the many lives touched by this amazing event in a small bird sanctuary tucked away at the edge of the Everglades, where ordinary people with extraordinary experiences found serenity and joy. Hundreds of people passed by this extraordinary view each day, gazing toward the high canopy with their own life stories unfolding.

Author D.K. Christi

About D.K. Christi

Amazon.com featured D. K. Christi as their "Author to Watch" stating, "D. K. Christi's debut novel, 'Arirang,' a romantic adventure that spans seven continents, conveys an underlying theme that 'life happens when you are planning something else.' In Christi's short stories such as *Chalk, The Magic Box* and *The Valentine*, exclusive to Amazon Shorts, themes of friendship surviving tragedy, love conquering adversity, and the triumph of the human spirit over the hardships of life serve to uplift and inspire. Discover a new voice in fiction and through her stories, perhaps discover something new about yourself."

Christi's short stories appear in numerous anthologies including two with L & L Dreamspell's "Romance of My Dreams" Anthologies I and II. "Ghost Orchid" is her first novel with L&L Dreamspell and takes the reader on a journey of mystery and ethereal beauty in the Everglades and exotic foreign locations that they will not soon forget.

Christi has spent much of her career living and working abroad where language and culture shaped her vision of the world and enriches her writing today. A polished platform speaker, she presents at national conferences with such diverse themes as multi-cultural diversity and embracing change. She writes and manages $multi-million grants from business proposals to marketing, but fiction is her passion. Originally from Michigan, Christi currently lives in Florida where she enjoys travel, dancing, kayaking, sailing and the Gulf. In her moments of melancholy, she fondly remembers three years of blue water sailing from Ft. Lauderdale to Venezuela with her family aboard *Lady Ace*.

"All I know is in this moment." …D. K. Christi